THE GREEK'S ONE-NIGHT HEIR

NATALIE ANDERSON

MILLS & BOON

First published in Great Britain 2020
by Mills & Boon, an imprint of HarperCollins*Publishers*
1 London Bridge Street, London, SE1 9GF

Large Print edition 2020

© 2020 Natalie Anderson

ISBN: 978-0-263-08459-7

MIX
Paper from
responsible sources
FSC™ C007454

For Evelyn the Awesome.

I could say it was because
you asked so nicely, but really
it's because you're amazing.

CHAPTER ONE

'YOU SHOULD BE RESTING, not worrying about me.' Theo Savas paced across the theatre foyer, working to keep his concern inaudible. He'd lived with his grandfather since he was ten and this was the first time in the last twenty years the old man had directly referenced something so personal. Revoking this rule wasn't just unsettling, it was unsafe. 'You've just come through a major operation—'

'And that's given me the opportunity to think. It's time, Theodoros. Your birthday is only a few weeks away.'

The lights above Theo flickered, signalling it was time for guests to take their seats, but he couldn't end this call without steering Dimitri back to unconcerned calm.

'Are you suggesting I'm getting old?' His joke was weak but he'd try anything to defuse his grandfather's escalating anxiety. Except anxiety was infectious and the vibes coming through the phone were making Theo's own muscles tense. That was in addition to the latent strain of the actual topic. 'There's plenty of time—'

'At this rate I'll never meet my great-grand-children—'

'You're not about to die,' Theo interrupted. He'd ensured Dimitri had been seen by the best specialists and they'd insisted that with quality rest Dimitri should recover well. 'You've years left in you.'

'I'm serious. You need to settle down...'

'And I will,' Theo reassured him softly and rolled his shoulders.

He ached to resist Dimitri's attempt to add yet another burden of responsibility, yet he couldn't brush him off.

Distantly he watched the ushers guide the last arriving theatregoers towards the doors. He needed to move if he was going to make it in there. He stepped forward but a whirlwind of a woman swept in front of him, cutting him off. The tall, slender tornado didn't stop to say sorry, indeed she didn't even see him screech to a halt to stop himself smacking into her. She just kept searching her cavernous handbag while racing towards the usher.

'How about Eleni Doukas? She's beautiful.'

Theo inwardly shuddered. Was Dimitri suggesting a woman for him?

'Don't you like very beautiful women?' Dimitri added.

Theo bit back a grimace. Sure, he liked women—beauty being only one of their attractions. But most women he met wanted vastly more than what he was prepared to give.

'Or Angelica.' His grandfather offered another contender for his consideration. 'She would be suitable. You've not seen her in years.'

Theo had reasons for that. Ironically they were the exact reasons his grandfather would probably welcome. Cultured, well-educated, perfectly connected Angelica had made it clear she'd accept marriage and produce four children while turning a blind eye to extra-marital affairs. But Theo would never be unfaithful and he'd never accept infidelity from his wife either. He knew too well the blisters, welts and scars that such affairs inflicted. The fact was that while Angelica had offered herself as the ultimate convenient wife, while it was the sort of arrangement Theo ought to accept, and while it was certainly what those in his milieu expected him to accept, the prospect of any matrimonial arrangement at all appalled him.

But Dimitri didn't need to know that.

'It has been a while…' Theo murmured, agreeing in order to soothe.

His gaze locked on the scene unfolding outside the theatre door. The blind-haste brunette was still rummaging in her bag. Unlike most of the women present, she wasn't wearing a shimmering gown. Instead black slim trousers encased her long, long legs. He focused on her feet and saw black flats—so, unaided by towering heels, that striking height was all her own? Interest rippled through him like the faintest breeze bringing relief on a hot summer's noon. She wore a black wool cardigan beneath which a grey blouse was buttoned to the neck. The dull combination gave nothing away of her figure, other than that she was slender. But it was her expression that pushed him closer.

She was still searching through her bag while casting desperate glances at the unmoved usher and as Theo neared he heard her talking endlessly in a hushed, frantic whisper. Was she trying to buy time? Faking her way in? She was doing a good job because she tugged something even in Theo's safely entombed heart. Her eyes glimmered with suspicious brightness and her cheeks paled as the doors further along from hers were shut.

'If not Angelica—'

'Arrange it,' Theo decisively interrupted Dimitri. The thought of some possible bride parade was crazy, but he'd consent just to give Dimitri something to look forward to.

He walked towards the pair standing at the last open door to the theatre. The woman had whitened beyond pale and interesting. Any more loss of blood and she'd faint. The honest entreaty in her expression lanced through him. Not faking. Mortified.

'Introduce me to your three top picks,' he authorised his grandfather.

'You're serious?' Dimitri wheezed.

'Yes.' Theo sighed, serious about meeting them, but not about marrying any. 'You're tired and worrying.' And the old man was bored with being bedridden. At the very least this would give him something satisfactory to think about for the rest of the evening. 'Make the arrangements.'

If it would settle the old man's pulse, then

he'd handle a couple of weekends being polite to houseguests. The nurse had warned his grandfather might experience a period of feeling low—apparently it sometimes followed life-saving surgery. Theo would do almost anything to lift his spirits.

'I'm flying home first thing so I'll see you tomorrow afternoon,' he said. 'We'll talk more about it then, I promise. I need to work now.'

'Good, Theodoros,' his grandfather muttered huskily. 'Thank you.'

Theo paused, an arrow of discomfort silencing him. Usually Dimitri was all steel—unblemished and immoveable, capably tolerating the burning heat of business, but today, in revealing his wishes for Theo to find a wife? Dimitri discussing *any* kind of relationship rang Theo's warning bell, reminding him that Dimitri was more vulnerable than he appeared. And his grandfather didn't need to thank him, Theo was the one who owed. Everything.

'It's all right.' He cleared his own husky throat. 'Sleep well.'

He ended the call and walked the last few paces of the foyer. As the main financial backer for this ballet production, he'd been given the best seat in the house. Which, if he wasn't mistaken, he'd just forfeited because the usher had closed the door with brutal finality.

If he'd walked a little faster, he might've made it but he was still distracted by that trouble in the form of a tall brunette. And he badly needed a moment of distraction.

'I'm so sorry.' She pleaded with the usher as she swept back behind her ear a tendril that had loosened from the long braid that hung down her back. Her eyes were very large and very worried and she desperately ransacked her bag yet again. 'I had it, I promise I had it—'

'I'm sorry, ma'am.' The usher stood, an impenetrable force, in front of the shut door. 'But without your ticket…'

Leggy Brunette's slender shoulders slumped. 'Yes, of course. It's just that…it was in here.' She searched her trouser pockets, then glanced around the floor as if somehow her ticket would materialise. 'I promise I had it…'

'Unfortunately it's too late.' The usher brusquely ended the conversation.

Hunching as if to hide, Leggy Brunette turned away, the curve of her pretty mouth dropping.

'Problem?' Theo stepped sideways, into her path.

She glanced up at him absently, then stopped dead. Her eyes widened and her second glance turned into a shocked stare. Theo happily stared back.

Her eyes were more than blue, they had a hint of pale purple, and he took another step closer on auto. 'You couldn't find your ticket?'

She shook her head and kept staring.

Theo couldn't hold back a small smile. Apparently she couldn't find her voice either. He was used to getting a reaction from women, but rendering one speechless?

At least some colour was flooding back into her face. But suddenly she swallowed and turned away. He couldn't resist following. She stopped at the nearest table and, amused, he watched as yet again she fruitlessly searched her bag. He caught a glimpse of something bulky in its depths, surely not a blanket?

'You know, they'll never let anyone in late,' he said softly to let her down gently. 'They won't interrupt the performance once it's begun.'

She dropped her hands and darted another glance at him. 'I know.' Her voice was adorably husky with her English accent soft and clear. 'It's just that I *had* it.'

And she *really* wanted to watch the ballet? Her

ticket loss was definitely genuine. Her sharp disappointment nicked his skin and the absurd desire to see her smile slid into his blood.

'Oh, Mr Savas.' The theatre usher suddenly appeared at his side, looking flustered. 'I can sneak you in if you'd like to follow me quickly...'

For a split second his eyes met those lavender-blues and he watched the consternation bloom within them.

'I wouldn't want to interrupt the rest of the audience,' he dismissed the usher's invitation smoothly. 'But thank you anyway.'

The usher beat a hasty retreat and Theo faced Leggy Brunette.

'No one gets in late unless they're ridiculously rich?' she muttered, soft reproach in her expression.

Uh... Yeah. 'I have a spare ticket you can use for the second half,' he murmured impulsively.

She looked away again as if the sight of him somehow hurt her unusual eyes. 'Um...' She fiddled with the strap of her insanely huge bag. 'That's really kind of you, but I couldn't.'

'Why not?' he asked. He wanted her to say yes and Theo was pretty used to getting what he wanted these days. 'It's a spare ticket,' he reiterated. 'You can still see the entire second half.'

Her hand twisted in the strap while more colour rose in her cheeks. He knew she was tempted, but wary.

'There's no trick,' he reassured softly. 'Just a ticket.'

She drew her lower lip between her teeth and bit down on it. 'Really?'

'Yes, really.' He chuckled. People didn't usually dilly-dally about taking things from him. 'It's not a big deal.'

That colour swarmed more deeply and she quickly glanced past him. 'You…don't have a date you're here with?'

Was *that* the reason for her incredulous expression? He suppressed another smile. 'No. Do you?'

'No.' She shook her head quickly.

Satisfaction surged with surprising force. 'Then I guess it's meant to be, right?'

'I…' She paused. 'Right.'

'And now we might as well have a drink while we wait, don't you think?' He nodded towards the gleaming theatre bar, his body thrumming with anticipation.

She turned to face him, her lavender eyes gazed directly into his and her chin lifted with a little pride. 'May I get you a drink, to say thank you?'

For a second Theo was bereft of speech. The women he dated never offered to pay. They knew him, knew how wealthy he was and they were happy to meld into his lifestyle. But his brunette in distress had no idea who he was and apparently had no desire to just take whatever she could from him.

'Please,' she added. 'I wouldn't want to feel indebted to you.'

Indebted by a mere ballet ticket? That thread of sensual awareness tightened. Was she worried he'd ask her to pay him back in some nefarious way? Well, she could remain calm, Theo had never needed to coerce a woman in his life. He might have money, but he wasn't spoiled and he'd never presume.

'Okay,' he said equably, but then couldn't resist teasing her prim dignity. 'But are you sure you have your wallet on you? You wouldn't want to make offers you can't fulfil.'

'Very funny.' Sparks lit her lavender eyes, but then her expression wrinkled. 'Damn it, you've made me need to check now.' She rummaged in her bag again—were those chopsticks in there? But then she extracted a small coin purse with a flourish. No sleek leather wallet filled with elite credit cards for her.

'I knew I had it,' she said victoriously. 'But I swear I had the ticket too.' She groaned ruefully. 'What an idiot.' A sudden little giggle bubbled out.

To his astonishment, his whole world narrowed until he saw only her—sparkling eyes and pretty lips and delight—and he found himself smiling back at her. Frankly it was the most he'd smiled in months.

'How about you go ahead and order?' he suggested huskily. 'I need a second to arrange the seat with the staff.'

'What would you like to drink?'

'You choose.' He shrugged. 'I'll have whatever you're having.'

'Are you sure you want to risk that?' she asked, her expression wrinkled again.

'Why?' He was surprised into another smile. 'Now I'm intrigued. Quick, go decide for the both of us.'

He couldn't resist watching her walk towards the bar. He really was intrigued—she was a contrary mix of shy and awkward and assured. Tall, slender, feminine and acutely refreshing. Just the tonic given the last two months of stress, isolation and uncertainty. But she was definitely cautious and perhaps she was right to be, given his inner temptation was to skip the ballet altogether and carry her back to his bed for the night. He'd worship those long limbs and work very hard to put a smile on her pillowy pout...

So not appropriate. Or normal. Not for him. He'd never followed in the footsteps of his playboy father and he never wanted to. He shook off that outrageous whisper of sin and strode towards the theatre staff. One drink, then it was back to duty.

When he walked back to the bar she was sitting all alone with two tall glasses in front of her and quite obviously trying not to appear self-conscious.

He placed the ticket on the bar beside the two drinks and lifted one. 'All arranged.'

He needed the drink. But on swallowing he quickly stifled his immediate grimace and subsequent smile. This sour fiery stuff wasn't quite the champagne he'd been expecting. At first glance he'd guessed she'd be a sweet romantic— sensitivity and shy awkwardness were obvious in her eyes. But then she came out with a line of soft-spoken sarcasm, a penchant for rocket fuel as an aperitif and a self-deprecating giggle that stole a rare smile from him.

'Thanks,' she said to him earnestly. 'That's so kind of you.'

Oddly he didn't want her to think he was *kind*. He wanted a bit more of a reaction than that. He wanted...he paused to battle the full force of what he wanted...but, yeah, it was pretty much everything he shouldn't want. It was everything illicit.

Leah Turner sipped her drink, stifling the urge to surreptitiously pinch herself. This kind of thing *never* happened to her. Somehow the most gorgeous guy had intercepted her during her most humiliating moment and gallantly turned her disappointment into something else altogether. And, man, he was gorgeous. Tall, lean, muscular, powerful, he exuded a sensual magnetism that was beyond normal. *She'd* most certainly never felt sexual attraction from one look. He was so dazzling it was hard to think and she wasn't sure what she was more rapt about—not missing the entire ballet, or stealing a few minutes of this man's time.

Because those eyes of his? Green eyes were usually a mix of colours—green mixed with blue or hazel, or bronze. But his were pure forest green. So rare, so startling, she had to constantly tell herself not to stare at him. She tried to stare at her glass instead, but only lasted a mere second before lapsing and gawping at him again. 'You're important around here?'

'No.'

She didn't believe him. She'd watched him speak with the theatre manager and that woman had been all deferential smiles and soothing words. He held more than charm. He held power. Hell, he'd made Leah feel as if she'd done *him* a favour by saying yes to taking the ticket.

He smiled and there was something a little dangerous in it. 'Why are you here alone?'

His accent curled her toes and made her an appalling cliché. She had no idea what the mix was, but it melted her like a lonely snowflake on a sunny windowsill.

'I'm not.' She lifted her chin. 'My friend is already here, but she's onstage.'

'She's a dancer?'

'Yes. She sent me the ticket but I was running late because I'd stopped to help Maeve with something.'

'Maeve?'

'One of the residents at the care home I work at. She's lovely and we bond over—' Leah paused, realising she was prattling. 'Over stuff,' she finished. He didn't need to know about her new job and the people she'd already fallen for. 'Why were you running late?'

'I was on a call.'

'Girlfriend problems?' she guessed, cheekily personal but it just had to be the case. 'Is that why you're alone? Did she stand you up?'

His eyebrows lifted in a quizzical look.

'What—you're never stood up?' she asked before thinking, *of course, he wasn't.*

'No girlfriend.' That gorgeous smile crept across his face as if he were pleased to be able to correct her. '*That's* the real problem. According to my grandfather anyway.'

'You were talking to your *grandfather*?' She was surprised. 'He wants you to settle down?'

He nodded mock seriously. 'And provide heirs to the family fortune.'

For certain there *was* a family fortune. His suit was so beautifully fitting it had to be tailor-made and the gleaming watch on his wrist screamed luxury style. 'You don't want to do that?'

'Not yet,' he said, obviously and unashamedly repelled by the idea.

'Yet?' she queried doubtfully because that wicked light in his eyes made her laugh. There was too much fun to be had first, clearly. How could he not be a playboy? All the women who'd want him, it'd be too easy. But she played along. 'Because you have too much to do? Too busy with work? Too many other options?'

'None of the above.' He chose another answer altogether. 'Hence no date to the ballet...'

'I don't believe you're out of options,' she said. 'You've *chosen* not to bring a date.' She cocked her head. 'Because you don't want to settle down at all?'

He met her gaze with knowing amusement.

She shook her head sadly. 'Why do I get the feeling your poor grandfather is going to be waiting a while...'

He rolled his shoulders and his amusement faded as something far more serious flickered in his eyes. 'He's been unwell—this is preying on him. Hence the lecture.'

Leah watched him blink away that sliver of pain. That he'd not ended the call soon enough to get into the theatre showed he had patience and loyalty and respect for his relative.

'Family expectations can be hard,' she offered with soft honesty. 'I'm an eternal disappointment to mine.'

He looked back into her eyes and they were held for a moment—silent scrutiny, total awareness—and she was struck by the conviction there was much more buried beneath his perfect surface.

'I don't believe you'd ever be a disappointment,' he finally muttered—so low and so serious that she couldn't smile and shake it off.

Instead a heated flush swept over her skin and she swallowed back the hard lump that had formed in her throat. 'Well, you'd be wrong.'

He gazed at her for another moment of that unspoken communication—the deeply guarded truth, not the superficial denial that there was anything wrong.

Then he blinked and his lips twitched. 'Your family want you to marry too?'

Laughter burst out, breaking that intensity. She shook her head.

'Quite right, it's a dreadful idea,' he teased.

'No,' she said firmly. 'It isn't—'

'You're wrong.' He saluted her with his drink again. 'All marriages end up miserable.'

'Wow...is that what happened to you?'

He almost choked on his drink and then laughed. 'Not married. Never married. Never will marry.'

Yes, the only ring in his world was the ring of finality.

'Because…' She inhaled deeply as she studied him thoughtfully. 'Parents?'

He flashed a look at her—pure pain, pure denial, pure promise of retribution.

'Yeah,' she murmured meekly. 'Poor grandfather.'

'You think I'm that predictable.' He took another sip.

'I think that everyone feels pain, sometimes,' she said. 'And often the people who inflict the most pain are the people we're meant to be closest to.'

'I'm not close to them,' he said softly, then forced another smile. 'So, tell me about your dancer friend. Is it her debut?'

'No, it's just that I've only recently moved to London so I haven't been able to see her perform until tonight.' She shifted guiltily on her chair as she remembered. 'And now I've missed her.'

'Only the first half. And she doesn't need to know you've missed that.'

'You think I should lie to her?'

He smiled at her as if she were a timid little lamb. 'You're omitting a little of the truth. That's not a lie.'

'Of course it's a lie,' she corrected him flatly. 'It's not completely honest.'

'And we should always be completely honest?' He shook his head and laughed openly.

'You think I'm wrong?'

'Naïve, perhaps.' He leaned closer. 'Sometimes telling the truth serves no purpose. When it can only hurt the person who has to hear it, why would you?' He broke off with a sharp breath.

She had the feeling he wasn't thinking of her little 'missing the first half' mistake any more.

'So you'd omit the truth, or tell a lie, to protect someone?' she asked.

'Of course.'

He said it with such quiet certainty, she knew he had and did. She thought of the grandfather all over again and wondered what it was he protected him from.

That quizzical look lit his eyes again. 'What would hurt your friend more? Knowing you missed the first half, or never knowing you missed it?'

'If she ever found out I *lied*, that would hurt her the most. But if I tell her the truth, she'll just laugh at me.'

He stilled, his gaze keen on her. 'And that doesn't hurt you?'

She shrugged. 'My crime isn't that critical and I'm already laughing at myself.' She eyed him.

'We can laugh together. Sharing pain takes some of the sting out of it, doesn't it?'

'Not always.'

'Hmmm.' She pondered it. 'The problem is, one omission inevitably leads to more lies—she'll ask what I thought of something in the first half and I'd have to lie then.'

'Or you could just not talk about it at all.'

She laughed. 'So your solution is to just bury everything and live in total denial? Pretend nothing bad ever happened?' She leaned closer. 'It'll only come back to haunt you.'

'Don't tell me you believe in ghosts.'

'Well, I believe some things—feelings mostly—can't stay buried. They rise like zombies and eat your brain to the point where you can't think clearly any more.' It happened to her frequently.

'So you always act on your emotions?' he queried. 'Act on gut feelings rather than with rational thought?'

She sighed. 'I'm human. I try to be a good one and not hurt others.'

'So honesty it is?'

'Ideally, yes.'

'Ideally.' He sent her an indulgent smile. 'So how, ideally, will your friend react?'

'I know she'll laugh. It's not the first time I've messed up.'

'You've known her a while?'

'We grew up in the same town and were in ballet class together.'

'But you don't dance any more?'

'My passion outweighed my talent.'

'Surely passion's the most important ingredient?' His eyes gleamed. 'Talent without passion is nothing. Skills can be learned, passion can't.'

'Well, that may be so, but I'm already taller than average.' She shrugged, long skilled at masking her self-consciousness about it. 'Put me in pointe shoes and I tower over most men.'

It wasn't the only reason she'd quit, but he didn't need to know anything more about her constant inability to meet her parents' expectations.

'Is that why you wear flat shoes now? So you're not taller than your men?'

Her *men*? She choked back a laugh at the thought. 'I wear them because they're comfortable. I dress to please myself, not some man.'

He grinned appreciatively. 'Sure. But you're not taller than me. You could wear high heels when we go out.'

'I'm not going out with you.'

'Aren't we out right now?' he teased.

She shook her head. 'By accident, not design.'

'So wouldn't you go out with me if I asked?'

'Would you ask?'

That smile hovered around his mouth and he took another sip. 'Perhaps it's better if I omit to answer—the truth might terrify you. It mildly terrifies me.' His gaze clung to her lips and radiated a flash of heat that rippled over her. 'What is it you like about ballet? The costumes? Because it's romantic?'

'There's nothing romantic about ballet,' she scoffed, covering that moment of awareness. 'It's ruthless.'

'You mean bloody blisters and sprained muscles?'

'I mean more than that. Did you know in this ballet the girl goes mad and dies of a broken heart because the man she loved *lied* to her,' she said with a pointed look. 'Because he *omits* to tell her he's betrothed to another woman. I don't think that's *romantic.*'

He chuckled but then leaned forward to tease. 'It was the prospect of marriage, see? It caused all the problems.'

She rolled her eyes even as she laughed. Just then theatre doors opened and the audience spilled out, shattering the sense of intimacy that had built between them. Somehow that time had sped by and she was sorry it had gone so quickly.

'It's probably time to take your seat.' He gestured behind her. 'You don't want to leave it too late...'

'Okay.' But the flutters in her stomach wouldn't cease. That she was going to spend the rest of the evening with him? Even though she knew he was just amusing himself, it was still unbelievable.

Leah followed the waiting usher, her pulse quickening as the woman guided her to the best seat in the theatre. Overcome with appreciation she turned to thank him, but he wasn't with them. Somehow he'd disappeared in the crowd. Too late she realised the truth. He wasn't sitting with her because it wasn't a *spare* ticket he'd given her. It was his own.

Disappointment hit as that unusual bubble of happiness and hope popped. She hadn't had the chance to thank him or even say goodbye. Instinctively she knew she wasn't going to see him again. Who said chivalry was dead?

But to think that for a second she'd thought he'd actually been attracted to her. She was mortified at the memory and glad he'd now gone, given he'd clearly just been filling in time.

As the lights dimmed it took a few minutes for her to appreciate the ballet but then Zoe appeared onstage and she was swamped with pleasure and pride for her friend.

After the final curtain call Leah walked to the artists' entrance at the back of the theatre to meet her and give her friend the gift she'd made. Her lost ticket confession resulted in them both giggling and then Zoe insisted Leah accompany her to the opening night company party to make it up to her. Secretly she wanted to escape home alone so she could remember her handsome stranger. Instead she smiled and said yes, ruefully thinking of him again as she omitted honesty to save her own embarrassment.

Theo Savas stalked out of the theatre, determined to resist the tempting whisper telling him to seek out that slender brunette with the hopelessly soft eyes. He forced himself to make the mandatory appearance at the ballet's opening night celebration. He couldn't skip it, given the party was at the hotel he was staying in. But he could escape early and have some space and privacy before his early flight home to Athens. He had little desire to socialise beyond the cursory showing of his face.

His mind teased, replaying the light conversation he'd had with the tall, ticketless sylph. He'd watched her from the distance during the ballet, happy in the back-row seat off to the side management had found for him. She'd sat motionless through the performance, apparently entranced, and she'd applauded energetically. But he'd seen a hint of sadness on her mouth when she'd turned to leave. Theo had pressed back into the crowd as competing instincts had warred within him. He had affairs only rarely—always discreet, always without strings, always unencumbered by emotion or the weight of baggage. There were no *hearts* involved in his dalliances. Physical pleasure was just a freely given gift—very simple, very satisfying. The suggestion of anything more was not. He'd seen the hurt it caused when it mattered too much.

And he didn't think the leggy brunette was the no-strings, no-hearts type.

As he walked into the reception room the nearest group of women turned to stare, then smile. One peeled off and walked over.

'You're Theo Savas.'

'I am.'

Invitation shone in the pretty dancer's eyes but he turned away from it as he invariably did. Yet he still couldn't shake the recollection of that brunette's lavender-blue gaze or the awkward interest that had shone from it. Regret curled.

'I'm—'

'I'm sorry,' he interrupted the woman briefly. 'I can't stop to chat.'

He'd check in with the company director and get out of here. But as he turned to seek out the director he spotted a tall figure on the other side of the room. His second glance morphed into a stare. And he smiled. Every sense sharpened. She was in shadow, but her silhouette was unmistakable. Triumph allowed temptation to burst free. His ticketless damsel must have been invited to the after-party by her dancer friend.

'Hey.' He caught her arm to get her attention in the crowd, barely quelling the impulse to pull her close.

'Oh...' Her pupils dilated as she stared up at him. There was no hiding the sensuality that sparkled in her eyes. 'What are you doing here?'

'I could ask you the same question.' He couldn't drag his hungry gaze from her face. It was as if he'd not seen her in months, not mere minutes. 'Where's your friend?' He didn't really care. All that mattered was that they had a second chance and he wasn't letting her slip away again. Not yet.

She glanced around then pointed to a petite woman animatedly talking to a group of dancers. 'Zoe's over there.' As she watched her that sparkle in her eyes dimmed. 'She's…busy at the moment.'

'She's left you alone.'

'You left me alone too.'

He stilled, silenced by that hint of reproach.

'She's having a good time' she added quickly, failing to mask her awkwardness in the sudden pregnant moment. 'She deserves to.'

'And you don't?'

'I did have a good time. But you gave me *your* ticket.' She looked up at him. 'Why did you do that? You missed the whole thing.'

He could omit a couple of little facts and bask in her gratitude, but he didn't want to lie to her. Not after that oddly intimate little conversation they'd had before the ballet. 'Actually, they gave me another seat, so like you I didn't miss the second half.'

That seat at the very side of the theatre had been perfect, because while it had given him an obstructed view of the stage, it had also given him an angled view of her...though that little fact he *was* going to omit.

'Oh, good. I'm so glad.' A faint wash of colour bloomed over her face. 'It was still very kind of you.'

'Mmm...' He still didn't feel very kind right now. He felt achy. 'It was my pleasure.' He'd enjoyed watching the emotions flit across her face. 'I get to go to the ballet a lot. The theatre, opera, sports fixtures...it comes with my job.'

'You don't enjoy it?'

'Sure. Mostly.' But when he had other issues pressing on his mind, not so much. And right now he had too much on his mind. It had been a miserable few months. He just wanted to forget it all for a while. Temptation beckoned. Maybe his method was standing right in front of him. And maybe, he just couldn't resist.

He held his hand out to her. 'Theo Savas.'

Leah didn't want to keep staring but she couldn't seem to tear her gaze away from him. 'Leah Turner.'

A premonition warned her, but the urge for the slightest touch was irresistible and she put her hand in his. For a second they were locked together in a moment of physical intimacy that felt much more powerful than a mere handshake should.

As she stared into his eyes her thoughts jumbled. He'd just been kind earlier—hadn't expected to see her again, hadn't known she was going to be at this party. His gift had been just that, a simple gift with no strings—just a thoughtful, generous moment between strangers.

But the banked fire in his gaze now? The sizzle shooting up her arm? The electricity short-circuited her brain. She couldn't look away from him. She couldn't release him any more than he could seem to release her.

'I should get going,' she mumbled.

'Why?'

She swallowed. 'I have work tomorrow.'

'So? I have a flight first thing.'

She couldn't help smiling. 'Is it a competition?'

'You tell me.'

She shook her head. 'I'm not a fan of competition.'

'No?' He nodded. 'No one likes losing.'

So true but she doubted he'd ever lost much.

'How about collaboration, then?' He was somehow closer. 'We'd work together to achieve a common goal...'

Her mouth was so dry she had to lick her lips before she could answer. 'And that goal would be?'

His eyes were serious even as his mouth curved into a wicked smile. Intensity beneath the charm. 'The best night of our lives.'

'Wow. Setting a big goal.'

'Always. If you don't aim high…' His smile faded as he studied her. 'I didn't expect to see you again.'

'Are you sorry you have?'

'I was sorry I didn't stay earlier. I was sorry I let you go.'

Her heart trembled. So why had he? She couldn't bring herself to ask. She still couldn't move either. Someone pushed past behind her, jostling her in the throng. He released her hand only to wrap his arm around her shoulder and draw her closer against his side. Just like that the rest of the world faded.

'You want to go somewhere quieter?' he asked.

Leah had never gone 'somewhere quieter' with anyone ever. But she knew what it meant. 'You barely know me.'

'And I'm not going to.' He smiled ruefully. 'I go back to Greece tomorrow.'

He was in town for only the one night. Was

he letting her know this would only be a one-time thing? Was she right in thinking there might even be a one time? She opted for diversion so she could process all the signals she was too inexperienced to be certain of. 'You're from Greece? Whereabouts?'

'Athens.' His gaze didn't waver—it was as if he knew she needed a moment to process. 'But I have a holiday home on an island.'

Of course he did. He probably had homes everywhere.

'Have you ever been there?' he asked, seeming to reach for the same delaying diversion she was.

She shook her head.

'No interest?' He looked aghast.

She laughed. 'I'd love to go there one day.'

'Sail around the islands, right?' He smiled as if it was what everybody wanted.

'I'm sure that would be amazing, but I'd really like to go to Delphi.'

'You studied Classics? The Antiquities?'

She shook her head. 'No, it's silly, but one of my favourite books was set in Delphi.'

'What book?'

'You probably haven't read it...'

'I'm actually quite well read—what's the title?'

She shook her head. 'It's an old paperback, you

won't know it…' She'd found it in the reception of the doctor's one time and smuggled it home and hidden it from her parents. A romantic suspense wasn't on the prescribed list her parents had drawn up for her.

He smiled, guessing that she didn't want to tell him. 'You'll have to travel there then, to see if it lives up to its literary imagining.'

'I've only just moved to London.' She shrugged. 'Greece might have to wait a while.'

'So you're new to town and I'm just passing through…yet fate has made it so we meet twice in the one night.'

'And you want me to…'

'Yes.' Something smouldered in his eyes. 'You know what I want you to do,' he said. 'I want you to come with me. And yes, I mean exactly what you're thinking.'

Yes, he'd changed. In the theatre, he'd held back for some reason. Now, he'd decided and he wasn't holding back at all.

'You're…not shy.' She bit her lip.

'But you are. Don't be afraid to go for what you want.'

She hovered—not indecisive, but insecure. 'I'm not good at this,' she confessed.

He didn't laugh at her. His expression was both

encouraging and strained. He lifted a hand and cupped her jaw, the soft touch silencing her.

'I'm not going to give you a report card, Leah,' he breathed, closer still. 'Anyway, there's no "good", only amazing. And for the record—so as not to omit any important details—I have no intention of either of us being hurt.'

There was a tension within him—a cause of worry or concern. For her?

'Want me to give you an example?' he asked in a husky whisper.

Her pulse thundered. She should pull back and say no. But she didn't want to and her body decided for her. She rose a half-inch on her toes and met his descending mouth.

Who knew a kiss could be so careful? It began as little more than a soft slide of his lips over hers. His fingers weaved into her hair at the nape of her neck as he held her loose but close. But then his other hand lifted to her waist, pulling her against his body, and the pressure of his mouth on hers increased, the intimacy intensified as he teased her with his tongue. With slow, devastating skill he inexorably pulled a deep response. Not just acquiescence and acceptance but action in return. He unsealed a vast yearning within her and something in her soul leapt—reaching for connection, commanding her to slide her hands up his firm chest to his broad shoulders…to *hold* him to her every bit as much as he was holding her.

But he stirred more than the heated blood and the sudden slick restlessness of her hips.

A burst of emotion burned careful right the way down to ruthless. Raw hunger was unleashed within—forced into revealing itself by the increasingly demanding counterpart within him. This wasn't just want, this was *craving*. She arched, opening for him—seeking more with her own touch, her own tongue and hands and press of her body. And he more than let her. His feet spread as he braced to take more of her in his hold and kissed her thoroughly—his strokes designed to soothe and torment at the same time. She knew it was crazy—that it didn't make sense—but there was something more than this delicious, uncontrollable lust between them. And it was this something more that made this undeniable.

She shook, violently trembling from head to foot, as sensation rampaged through her like a river released from a decades-locked dam.

At her shudder he ripped his mouth from hers.

'What do you think?' His breathing was so roughened his speech sounded slightly slurred.

Thought had very little to do with it. She gazed up, relieved he'd not released his hold on her because she felt dizzy. She drank in the light flush on his skin and the glittering depths of his eyes—basking in the possessive focus he bestowed on her. Still pressed tightly against him, she felt not only his physical desire, but his restraint. She knew he'd walk away from her if she wished.

But that other ache welded her to him, that hidden, true, tender need. His reasons were no doubt different from hers, but she felt his loneliness ran as deep. For the first time she was compelled to both give and take of something unequivocally intimate.

Her answer was so simple, so easy. She couldn't let this rare moment go. She couldn't let *him* go.

'I think I'm coming with you.'

CHAPTER TWO

His smile was a blazing mix of triumph and sensual determination and barely hidden relief. She realised he was as delighted and as dazed as she was and somehow that multiplied the myriad want and need and hot mess of yes within her.

'I can't leave without saying goodbye to Zoe,' she muttered.

'Of course.' He escorted her through the crowd, stepping back when they came up to her friend.

'Sorry, Zoe.' Leah caught her attention. 'I'm going to call it a night—'

'Since when do you know Theo Savas?' Zoe interrupted her, managing to screech and whisper at the same time. 'Since when does Theo Savas kiss anyone in public like that?'

'You saw...just then?' Leah's body smoked with embarrassment.

'OMG, yes, go.' Zoe laughed and pulled her into a quick, tight hug. 'You must, just, *go*. Do everything I would and more,' her friend whispered in her ear. 'For heaven's sake, have some fun for once!'

Leah's pulse hammered as Theo firmly grasped her hand and led her through the crowded function room and into the sudden silence of the hotel corridor. She was floating, not walking, right? In the elevator he glanced down at her and smiled but she saw the question in his eyes and tension in his body.

She felt the question too—since when did *she* wander off with a complete stranger? Before tonight she'd never considered it, would never have thought she *would*... Yet he didn't feel like a stranger, more of a kindred spirit—as complicated and careful, those layers of responsibility and obligation hiding other needs and wants. She'd do all she could for someone she cared about; that he did too struck a chord—as if they were vibrating in harmony even though there could be nothing more than this one night between them. And then there was that sheer physical response that she just couldn't release herself from.

She'd never done anything adventurous, nothing reckless or fun either. She'd spent so long trying to please her parents and fit in with their impossible standards and it was past time to have one night just for her. She wanted to share it only with him.

He unlocked the door of his hotel suite and she stepped inside. The drapes didn't cover the tinted windows and the London skyline was like fairy lights. She turned and took in the rich interior—pure luxurious space and decadence. But then Theo stood in the centre of it and the sumptuous background faded away. He was like a sun god—casting everything else in shadow.

She couldn't be the first woman to fall completely beneath his spell but she was quite calm about that. She felt too pleased to have seen him again and realise that he was—amazingly—attracted to her too.

'Do you do this all the time?' she asked, too fascinated to think before asking.

'Not as often as you're thinking.'

She wasn't sure she *was* thinking any more—she was still floating on that gravitational pull right towards him. 'I don't do this, ever.'

'Never ever?'

She shrugged as embarrassment heated her skin. She wasn't going to tell him he was with a woman no other man had ever chased. A woman crippled by an inferiority complex bigger than Jupiter. What did it matter what she'd done or not done before? Right now there was this and it was too powerful to ignore. She wanted more of his touch—of that connection and elation when he'd kissed her. More than seduction, more than madness, it was an ache unlike anything she'd known burning low in her belly. Its searing intensity rapidly escalating until it seemed to singe her inside and out, leaving her breathless because of this urgent, unstoppable need to touch.

'I should offer you a drink or something.' He ran his hand through his hair and huffed out a breath as if he too were struggling to recover.

It seemed imperative to feel again that need that mirrored her own. 'I'm happy with just the "or something",' she mumbled shyly.

He looked startled for a second, then smiled. He moved towards her—graceful, powerful, careful. 'I wanted this from the moment I saw you.'

She jerked her head, negating the compliment because she was unable to believe him. 'You don't have to tell me…nice things.'

Something flickered in his expression. 'You're not used to people telling you the truth? You're beautiful, Leah. Robbed me of my self-control in seconds.'

She closed her eyes. She didn't want to listen—didn't want words to destroy her belief in this moment. But then she sensed he was close. She could feel his heat and his tension.

'If I don't have to tell you,' he whispered softly right in her ear, 'then I'll *show* you.'

A paralysing desire took hold at the sound of his determined promise. She half expected a furious onslaught of passion—she would have welcomed that too. But it wasn't.

It was slow, delicious torture. Another slow kiss—easing her back into his arms. Every touch not only a tease, but a celebration of her. Making her breathless, making her move closer, making her want something she couldn't articulate. As she trembled, he picked her up and carried her through to the bedroom and set her down on the big bed.

She shrugged out of the cardigan and then he took over, unbuttoning then peeling the blouse from her body. He paused to gaze at the white bra beneath, then undid it, pulling away the little lace cups that covered her small breasts, and he groaned. Not judging her but enjoying her. Not disappointed, but delighted. There was nothing to be had here but pleasure. She felt a reckless safety in his arms. No one had kissed her like this. His touch silenced anxious thought and she let herself be carried away by the basic instinct of her body—caving in to the demand to shift closer, to move with him and torment him back. He unzipped her trousers and slid them down, lifting her feet to slip her shoes from them at the same time.

'Scarlet silk.' His hot laugh tickled against her skin as he roved back up her body, lingering over her hips. 'That I didn't expect.'

'What did you expect? White cotton granny pants and a chastity belt or something?'

He laughed again and bent to kiss her upper thigh, nibbling on the edge of the silk as he went.

Leah moaned. Truth was, this was the first pair of sexy undies she'd bought herself. Even then she couldn't get it right and wear a matching bra. But she hadn't wanted her bra to be visible beneath her blouse, so she'd gone with white.

'It confirms a theory I've been developing about you,' he murmured.

'And what's that?' She could hardly string the words together.

'That you're more sensual than you appear… you've been hiding your true scarlet self.'

'You're reading too much into it—they were the first I grabbed from the drawer.'

'Because you have a drawer *full* of scarlet silk?'

She couldn't reply. *Where* was he kissing her... slowly inching along the waistband of those scarlet panties? Secrets and desire swamped her and she was shy about the fact that he'd discovered something she'd barely recognised within herself. She'd bought the one pair because it had been all she could afford. It had taken so long to choose which one; she'd wanted them all. Her secret enjoyment of them wasn't so secret now. She shivered.

'You "don't do this, ever", Leah?' He paused and looked back up to her eyes.

She didn't want to lie to him. She didn't want to hold anything back, but it was hard to push the answer past the lump in her throat. 'No.'

As he nodded it occurred to her that he already knew the answer. He'd been able to *tell*?

A slither of mortification chilled her skin. 'Does that bother you?'

'No.' He lifted himself up to lie beside her and searched her features. 'But are you sure you want me to be your first one-night stand?'

The reminder that that was all he was offering didn't bother her. But his blunt question revealed he hadn't realised the entire truth about her. Where he meant one night, she meant ever at *all*.

She nodded, her voice stolen by shyness and the fear that if she told the truth he'd stop. The last thing she wanted was for him to stop.

He kissed her mouth. His hand teased one breast, then the other, then rubbed firmly down her stomach, slipping beneath the waistband of those scarlet panties. At her shocked gasp, his kisses deepened. But he didn't stop his hot exploration—his fingers delving lower, stroking where she was most sensitive, discovering for himself her most secret place.

With every lash of his tongue, of his fingertips, the last of those knots holding her in reserve loosened until she was totally undone. Reduced to nothing but heat and light, pliable in his hands, she didn't just let him touch all he liked, she hungered for it—writhing like an animal. She arched, seeking more caresses, parting her lips to invite another deep kiss—her tongue tangling with his, her hand clawing his shoulder in an aching invitation to come closer.

'Yes,' he praised her in a gravelly voice as she moaned in desperation.

His fingers slid, his thumb strummed and his mouth sealed over hers again—stoking her until she went beyond burning and tumbled into total meltdown.

Time stopped as her hips bucked and she rode his hand. In those lost moments, there was nothing else in her world but him, in the escalating rhythm and depth of plundering touch. She tautened for one last infinite moment of torment and then his attention finally tore her apart. She screamed as ecstasy hit in a wave that smashed her to pieces.

Theo rubbed his forefinger back and forth along the waistband of her panties, lightly toying with her while she recovered from the most beautiful orgasm he'd had the pleasure of giving. He ached to strip her free of them and plunge into her hot, tight body. But her comment that her panties ought to be white replayed in his mind. White was the colour of innocence. And she'd joked about a chastity belt? He'd been too far gone for that to register properly. He glanced up at her face and recognised the gleam of resurging desire in her eyes. But there was shyness as well and the slight wariness—of a novice?

A weight of warning pressed low on his spine. He levered up from the bed and didn't break free of her gaze as he shucked his tie and swiftly unbuttoned his shirt. Her lips parted as she stared, avidly watching as he stripped. As his hands went to his belt buckle she stilled. Impatient, he shoved both his trousers and boxers down, revealing his bulging erection and watching intently for her reaction. She couldn't resist looking—couldn't take her eyes off him—but they widened in shock and he saw her swallow. And as he stepped back to the bed her breathing quickened.

'This isn't just your first one-night stand, is it?' he asked, his voice harsher than he could control.

Her eyes widened more and he knew he had to ask the follow-up.

'Are you a virgin, Leah? Is the "never ever", actually never *anything*?'

She bit her lip and insecurity flashed.

'How could you not tell me?' He knew he was right—her reaction to his nudity said it all.

Her face filled with a fiery sweet warmth that scorched his soul—he couldn't turn away from her even when he probably should.

'How could you tell?' she asked.

'It was your comment that these ought to be white. And the chastity belt?' He stroked the scrap of scarlet silk that would now be the only barrier between them.

That rosy bloom of embarrassment spread over every inch of her pale skin. 'Do you want me to leave?' She was very still but her hands formed into fists at her sides.

'No.' Raw hunger clawed more savagely within him, but he was determined to resist—to do what was right here. 'Why didn't you want to tell me?'

'I didn't want you to stop.'

The hint of wounded look in her eyes smote what had been—until tonight—an impenetrable heart. 'I won't stop if you don't want me to.'

She gazed into his eyes. He saw the trust. He saw the need. He vowed not to let her down.

'Let's just play, okay?' he clarified. 'We don't have to…'

'Do everything?' She swallowed. The glimmer of disappointment was so obvious in her lavender eyes.

'Decide right now.' He bent and kissed her, unable to stand the droop of disappointment on her full, lush mouth. And at first touch he sank back onto the bed, unable to resist getting as close as he could to her. He'd make her come again, he'd taste her, there was so much they could still do; there were so many other ways to fulfil the need savaging its way through his limbs.

She was revelation all over again. He lost himself in the sensation, the warmth and pleasure of touching her. He removed her silky scarlet panties so slowly, tormenting them both. And then he kissed her, tasting her there, teasing her with his tongue until he had to grip her hips hard to hold her still as she succumbed to her next orgasm.

Her screams suspended time. Bewitched, he let her push him onto his back. He pulled her above him. But with every slow second that he savoured as she blanketed him with her soft slender body, the yearning to have her completely deepened. Recklessness rose within him because she wasn't holding back at all. Untutored but unashamed, her hips circled against his, the tight, delicious rub of her nipples scored his chest so degree by degree his, oh, so noble desire to hold back lessened.

It was as if he'd unlocked a simple, small box only to discover it opened into myriad compartments...each like a room full of willingness and warmth. The depths of her response, her abandon, became unreserved. He stilled at the smoky curiosity in her gaze and the unconscious seeking sweep of her hands over him. She wanted touch. She wanted to explore her sensuality, through him. How could he deny her?

She tracked her fingertips down his abs. Unable to stay relaxed, every muscle tensed with desire as she tracked lower. He ached for her to cup him. His erection strained higher, he felt the searing tightening in his balls, the urge to thrust against her palm rushed. He licked his lips because his mouth was parched and holding back now was almost killing him.

'Do you want me to kiss you?' she asked softly.

He wanted anything. Everything. He blinked.

She smiled, a burst of pleasure in her eyes. 'Want me to help you find your tongue?'

Heat strained his body. That playful whisper knocked once more on his well-entombed heart. 'You don't have to...'

'Did you feel you had to for me?' She looked up at him, shyness glimmering in her eyes as she whispered huskily.

'No,' he sighed, unable to form complete sentences. 'Wanted to.'

'I can't want to?'

He swallowed and gave in. 'Go right ahead.' With a groan he closed his eyes, desperate to summon self-control as he felt her breath on him.

She cupped him and it was sweet torture.

'Oh.' She looked at him as he flinched. 'Can I—?'

'Do anything. Anything you want. Just don't stop.' His breathing roughened.

She didn't stop. He watched, all his senses

sharpened and arrowed on her. She was stunning—her long hair had loosened, tumbled about her shoulders, her long, lean, pale limbs unfolded around him. Her mouth was on him. Her mouth—

'Stop. *Stop.*' He dragged in a harsh breath.

She froze and pulled back with a worried expression. 'I'm sorry—'

'No.' He rubbed his forehead with a hard hand and groaned. 'It's just... I'm going to come.'

'Don't you want to?'

His shout of laughter hurt. His whole body ached. 'I wanted to warn you—'

'I don't want to stop,' she whispered.

The desire in her eyes stiffened him impossibly more. He growled his assent, unable to form another word, his want was too great. And then she sucked him dry.

His heart pounded so loud he thought it was going to burst. When he could finally open his eyes, he saw her smiling down at him—pride and amusement gleaming in her gaze. She was energised and so beautiful. She wasn't just insatiable, but capable of experiencing an intensity he knew was rare. And of sharing it with that gorgeous little laugh of hers.

'You okay?' He didn't know why he was asking her when he was so light-headed he wasn't sure he'd ever be able to sit up again. But then adrenalin fired him anew. Because he realised she was incredibly aroused. She'd liked touching him, tasting him. Getting and giving pleasure was always a great way to spend a night, but this was something else. This felt sweeter and sexier than anything.

'I still don't want to stop,' she said in the softest whisper. 'I still don't want you to stop.'

Her confession just demolished him. He was unable to resist and desperately aching to please her—wanting her to be more than sated, more than thrilled. He didn't want to deny her anything. So when he should've been spent, he was hard again and filled with an arrogant, outrageous determination. Who was he to tell her what she should or shouldn't do anyway? She knew he was leaving in the morning. She knew there was only this between them, only now. And she'd given them both permission to make the most of it. All he wanted now was to make it the best he could for her. Which meant keeping himself in check for a while yet. And being certain.

'I've never slept with a virgin before, Leah,' he said hoarsely, still catching his breath.

Her lashes veiled her eyes. 'Not even when you were a virgin?'

'No, I wasn't the first for my first. Do you really want to talk about—?'

'Did she make it good for you?'

A wry smile curved his lips. 'She did.'

'Then maybe think of this as paying it forward?' She looked as if she was braced for rejection.

He just couldn't deny her. 'You know you can change your mind. I'll—'

'Theo—'

'I don't want to hurt you,' he confessed rawly. It was incredibly true. Somehow, this woman he'd met only a few hours ago was precious to him. She mattered.

Her expression softened. 'If it hurts, maybe you can kiss it better...' She trailed off, suddenly shy.

That wave of protectiveness welled in him. He turned, swiftly searching the bedside table drawers. Relieved, he tossed the small box he'd found onto the bed. He'd leave nothing to chance.

Leah moaned as he pressed kisses across her collarbones and down her décolletage. He was so patient—too patient really. When he finally braced above her, anticipation heightened to a new level. He was big and heavy and wonderful. The slick hot reality impinged as she saw his muscles bunch. He braced as he held back. She knew he was being careful; she could tell in the way he watched her so closely. His concern melted her all the more.

'Please,' she murmured, knowing he needed to hear her wish again.

His expression tensed and he moved. Leah gasped as his big body invaded hers—tearing that last tiny barrier to bury deep inside her. He caught her sharp cry in a quick kiss.

'Sorry,' he muttered. His gaze was filled with searching concern for her. Of course that compassion was there—because if it wasn't she never would have sought this with him.

'Are you okay?' He framed her face and kissed her again and again—so gentle and lush.

He was pressed so deeply into her. So incredibly close. And it was so overwhelming she could only nod, as she adjusted to his possession and to the millions of nerve endings that had sparked to life within her—that suddenly sought so much more.

He held firm, slowly kissing her until the stillness was too much for her—she needed him to move. Warmth overflowed. She'd not expected it would be this intimate and yet of course it was. She revelled in the tender passion of his kisses and her body relaxed until she was no longer just accepting his invasion, but welcoming it—slickening, heating, until she instinctively rocked her hips to help. He kissed her again and his groan reverberated into her chest. He moved then too, taking control, making it magic, and she completely forgot that first moment of pain in her building delight. She followed his rhythm, learning this dance until instinct urged her to hold him closer still. She wrapped her arms and legs around him, clinging close with every part of her as the spasms of delight snuck up on her so swiftly.

'Don't stop,' she breathed desperately. 'Please, don't stop.'

But as she curved more tightly around him, so close to completion, he growled and suddenly froze.

'Theo?' she asked.

'Trying...' he gulped a breath '...not to be too rough.'

But she needed *all* of him.

'Finish me,' she begged.

At her broken plea she felt his restraint unravel and power surged in his body. He lost it—thrusting harder and faster and it was so dizzying, so intense, so unbearably good. She could only try and hold on, but her restraint had fled too. She clawed his skin, grasping him as tight as she could in her grip as her body and mind locked on him. But he didn't stop, he pounded closer and fiercer, pushing them higher, further and faster until everything exploded in a flash of heat and light and utter, utter ecstasy.

Hours later Leah blinked, wishing she'd eaten more carrots as a kid so her night vision was better. Instead, she tripped over her shoe and muffled her squawk of pain as she hopped and tried to see well enough to find her other one. Her clothes had been scattered on the floor around the bed and, while she'd found most of them, she just needed this one last thing.

'Why are you trying to sneak out?' The lazy tease in his voice made her shiver.

'Sorry.' She stifled her nervous laughter.

As he switched on the lamp she glanced at him, embarrassment curling her spine. 'I didn't mean to wake you.'

His eyebrows lifted. 'Because you didn't want to talk to me?'

She swallowed. 'I just...'

His low chuckle filled the void. 'Relax. This doesn't have to be awkward.'

'No?' But she needed to escape now because the temptation to fling herself back into bed, wrap herself around him and never let him go was just a little too strong.

He leaned out of bed and reached for his phone. 'Give me your number.'

She stilled; the crowd of clamouring emotions shaking her up needed to settle. 'I don't think that's a good idea,' she said bravely. The night was over, the magic gone—wasn't it? 'We don't even live in the same country.' She drew in a breath. 'So…there's no point, is there?'

She wanted him to argue with her and say he wanted to see her again. But she had the feeling she'd spend the rest of eternity hoping he'd call. And if he did? Would she end up his booty call when he was in London? He didn't want a relationship, and never marriage, remember? And she did want those things. So this needed to stay as a finite dream night.

'No point?' he echoed quietly.

She turned away as he got out of bed and scooped his trousers up from the floor. She couldn't see his body again, couldn't stop to talk more. If only she'd not fallen over her shoe she'd be out of here by now. It had been great sex, that was all. Other people experienced this all the time. She couldn't be all inexperienced and needy now.

'At least let me get you home safely.'

She couldn't resist glancing back at him. 'I'll be fine on the—'

'I'm only going to phone down to the porter and order you a cab.' He sombrely studied her with those intense eyes. 'I wasn't going to drive you myself. I have to get to the airport, remember?'

'Okay, thanks.'

But her heart pounded appallingly quick and hard as he strolled towards her and made it impossible to think.

She couldn't look away. He was extraordinarily beautiful. Bronzed skin, strong, sleek muscle. She couldn't believe she'd had the privilege of touching him *everywhere*. She swallowed, clawing back the desire to do it again right now.

She couldn't possibly kiss him goodbye but just walking away seemed rude. For lack of a better idea she held out her hand for him to shake before he got too close. He paused, as if debating whether to take her hand or do something else entirely.

'No regrets, Leah?' he asked softly, finally clasping her hand in his in a handshake like no other. Could he feel her thundering pulse through her skin?

'None.' She couldn't get her voice above a whisper. 'But it's done.'

'Okay. Then, bye, beautiful Leah.' He glanced down at their linked hands for a brief moment and then released her. 'Thank you for a wonderful night.'

'Thank you too,' she echoed awkwardly and quickly turned away. 'Bye.'

On the way down to the ground floor she squared her shoulders and refused to feel any sadness. *Refused.* She'd had an amazing night—the best night of her life, just as he'd promised. As she acknowledged that, a surprising shot of confidence lifted her. So what if she had bed hair? So what if the porter waiting to escort her into the taxi could tell she'd spent the night barely sleeping because one man—one *amazing* man—had wanted her and she'd wanted him and together they'd done all kinds of wonderful?

Things were looking up. She'd moved to London, she had her own place, a new job she actually wanted and she was going to make such a go of it.

Finally, her life was only going to get better.

CHAPTER THREE

'WHAT DO YOU think of this pattern, Leah?'

Smiling, Leah paused by the open doorway of her favourite resident's room. She loved her job as receptionist in the private care facility in North London—mainly because she loved the residents. They were interesting and she enjoyed, not only being able to help them and their families, but just talking to them too. She'd been here coming up five months and as her confidence had increased, her bond with them all had built.

Now she went into Maeve's room to study the paper the old woman was holding up to her. They'd discovered a kindred fondness for knitting early in Leah's employment. It was a favourite way of relaxing, aside from reading, for them both. So Leah looked at the picture with interest. It was a pattern for a baby jacket. She'd thought Maeve's grandchildren were all older. Perhaps there was going to be a great-grandchild?

'I thought I'd better get started for you, but wasn't sure which colour you're going to need. Have you found out? Should I do pink or blue?' The elderly woman's eyes twinkled with curiosity.

Startled, Leah let out a stunned little laugh. Maeve wanted to knit this for *her*? *Why?* 'I'm not pregnant, Maeve.'

'You're just the right age to be pregnant,' Maeve said. 'I was about your age when I had my first.'

Leah laughed again—was this a sweet case of wishful thinking? 'I'm sorry, Maeve, but—'

'You can't fool me, you know. I know it's the norm these days not to say anything until you're a few months gone, but you can't hide how radiant you are now. You have so much more colour and sparkle than when you first started.'

Leah's breathing quickened. Did she? That was because when she'd started, she'd only just moved away from her parents. It had taken a while to bounce back from the pressure they'd put on her for so long and to accept that what she wanted to do with her life wasn't anything they'd ever approve of.

'I'm on a health kick,' Leah explained, because

that was true. She'd been eating well and exercising…it wasn't anything else. It couldn't be.

'You don't drink coffee any more,' Maeve pointed out, looking very pleased with herself. 'Because you're blooming.'

Leah stared at the older woman and slowly shook her head again. But inside she was beginning to panic. She *had* become sensitive to certain smells and tastes, but that was because she'd chosen to eat so well—wasn't it? It was impossible for her to be pregnant because she was single and she'd never—

'Leah?'

'I think the pattern looks beautiful.' She forced a quick smile. 'I just need to…um…' Her brain wouldn't compute. She couldn't think of a reason to leave—she just threw another smile at Maeve and dashed from the room.

Oh. Leaning against the wall in the corridor outside, she breathed hard. For the first time in for ever she thought of that magical night. She'd been trying to forget it—to move on and not judge every man she passed by the impossible standard that was Theo Savas. Of course, no one compared. That night had been part of the reason her confidence had grown too. But for her to have got *pregnant*? She couldn't have. He'd used protection each time—she'd seen him. And that night had been months ago and she'd had her period since, right?

Oh, no. She put her hand to her mouth as she frantically tried to think, but the panic zombies had eaten her brain. She'd always had an irregular cycle and she'd been so busy she hadn't been paying attention to that much because she'd thrown herself into her work in part to help herself forget *him* and now she couldn't remember...

Oh, no, no, no. Cold horror curdled her blood. What Maeve had noticed was true. She suddenly loathed the smell of coffee. And her skin was kind of amazing in a way it had never been before. And now she remembered other things she'd not realised before—that tiredness that had leached her for a while a few weeks ago? She'd attributed it to getting used to life in London with all the commuting and everything, but what if it had been symptomatic of something else?

Impossible. It just had to be impossible. Please could it be impossible?

But what if...? The appalling possibility took hold. She was so terrified she couldn't concentrate at all on her work. For the first time she left the second her shift was over, and stopped by a pharmacy on her way home. Once she was alone in her tiny apartment, her hands trembled as she opened the pregnancy test.

Even doing this was ridiculous, right? In a few minutes she'd be giggling about wasting her money. There was no way she could be pregnant. The idea was just a farrago of fact and fantasy planted by a confused elderly woman and taken on by her because she had some random make-your-skin-glow fever…right?

Two minutes later bright blue stripes appeared on the white background.

No, no, no, no, no.

Leah stared stupidly at the positive result. It couldn't be correct. It just couldn't. *How* could she be pregnant?

Her zombie mind now zinged with endless un-answerable questions. Where had the morning sickness been? Or all the other symptoms? More importantly, what was she going to do? And most terrifyingly, how was she going to tell *him*?

All these months she'd been trying not to ob-sess over him like some loser stalker. Now she had to make contact. How was she going to do that? And how on earth was he going to react?

Please, no.

With shaking hands she used the second test in the box. And cried when she got the same result. She picked up her phone and begged her way into a last-minute appointment with an after-hours doctor who was able to give her a scan to check on the baby's development. Leah stared at the grey whirls of motion on the screen as they formed into an image that made her eyes smart. Tiny and perfect. And *terrifying*.

Apparently everything was just as it should be for just over four months gestation. Everything appeared healthy and normal and all she had to do was keep eating well and taking care of herself.

'Would you like me to phone someone for you?' The attending nurse smiled at her as the doctor left the room. 'You've gone very pale.'

'No, thank you,' Leah murmured, standing up to leave. 'I'm fine. I'm often pale.'

'If you're sure…?' The concern didn't leave the nurse's eyes.

'Yes,' she said, aching to get out of there. 'Thank you anyway.'

Back alone in her apartment, she folded her legs beneath her on the sofa and tried to come up with a plan, except all she could do was hunch in a disbelieving ball.

She had to tell him.

Truthfully she'd searched for him online

months ago in a moment of weakness just after their one night together. She'd even avoided seeing Zoe much because she couldn't bring herself to share a moment of that night with anyone. She'd discovered Theo Savas was regarded as Greece's most eligible bachelor. Heir to a business banking empire that had branches around the world—he was now CEO and game-changer of that enterprise and apparently he could do no wrong because he'd broadened the family holdings, buying diverse companies and creating a conglomerate of success. There wasn't a hint of scandal about him—he wasn't known for partying ways, no rolling parade of beautiful girlfriends in the media, no salacious rumours of his endless succession of one-night stands.

But he had them. He was just discreet and courteous and too clever to leave a woman dissatisfied…

He was going to be horrified. But as much as she really didn't want to, she had to tell him. The question was *how*. Not for the first time she regretted not taking his phone number. Until today those regrets had been tempered by the knowledge she'd saved herself from making a complete idiot of herself by begging him for another night. That wasn't how Theo Savas rolled. He was too busy being the banking CEO, the charitable gift-giver, the employer of many, sponsor of the arts… He was too busy being perfect.

Would he even remember who she was?

She searched him again on her phone. His company's main headquarters were in Athens and there was another office in London, more in other cities around the world. But there was no email address for him—only a public contact address. She couldn't put something this personal into an email that would be read by an administrative assistant. She'd have to phone.

She tried the Athens branch first.

'I'm sorry, do you speak English?' Leah asked the woman who answered in rapid Greek.

'Of course.' The woman's reply was professional and immediate. 'How may I help you?'

'I'd like to speak to Theo Savas, please.' Leah tried to sound confident and assertive but her nerves were fluttering so hard they rendered her breathless.

'May I ask who is calling?'

'Leah.' She cleared her throat, wincing at her own rushed answer. 'It's important I speak with him.'

There was a pause. 'Mr Savas is very busy. May I ask what it is in regards to?'

'I…' Leah braced as a wave of hot embarrassment swarmed over her skin. 'It's a personal matter.'

There was an even longer pause. 'If it is a personal matter, then you will know Mr Savas's personal number on which to contact him.' The woman's tone was cruelly cool.

Mortified, Leah hung up in a flash.

Why did he need such a dragon-led first line of defence? Did he have women trying to get in touch with him all the time?

Probably, she realised morosely. And the brutal fact was her pregnancy would appal him. He wasn't ready to settle, even if his grandfather wanted him to. And neither he nor his grandfather would want him to have a child with some random one-night stand. He moved in exalted circles—his clients were CEOs, royals, celebrities—he'd be expected to marry and have a family with someone from the same social strata. That wasn't her. She was utterly unsuitable—not educated, not successful, not glamorous or gorgeous… She faced the reality. She wasn't anything he'd either need or want. And she couldn't bear to think of her child knowing it was an unwanted disappointment to its father.

She was that to her parents.

Nor could she contact her parents and ask for their help. She gently held her lower abdomen as she briefly considered, then dismissed, the possibility. This precious baby deserved protection. It deserved to be loved and secure and never to face the judgment of her impossible-to-please parents. She wanted her child never to experience that inferior feeling she'd had all her life. She might not have much else, but she had unlimited love and support to offer her child. And she had to do the right thing for it.

She had to get in touch with Theo to at least give him the chance to consider how, or if, he wanted to be involved in their baby's life.

She glanced down at the website she'd pulled up with its list of addresses and phone numbers. What if she went to his London office and spoke with someone there? If she could convince them how important it was that she speak with Theo directly? But how could she convince them? She shrivelled with embarrassment at the thought of telling a stranger anything of that intimate night, but she had no choice.

The next morning Leah stood on the other side of the street from his London office and watched the people come and go from the building. All were smartly attired—exactly the opposite of her in her old wool coat with her home-made cardigan and her patched black jeans beneath. Her legs trembled and she pulled her coat more tightly around her and made herself step inside the lobby.

The place was beyond intimidating with its sleek interior. She looked at the perfectly coiffed women at the counter and just knew she'd get the same response as she'd got from the Athens receptionist. She'd be exposed in front of all these smooth professionals who were giving her sideways looks as it was. She didn't fit in here—she knew it, they knew it. She didn't have the money, looks or status.

Why had she refused to give Theo her number? Why had she refused to take his? Why had that contraception failed?

She felt too fragile to cope with public scrutiny and rejection. But as she glanced around, she realised her hesitation had caught the attention of the security guard. He was staring at her, unsmiling. All those old feelings of insecurity and inferiority burned. She was so out of place— *again*. She wasn't good enough—she was *never* good enough. Humiliated, hurting, scared, Leah pushed forward and went up to the counter. This wasn't about her. This was about her baby.

'I'd like to get in touch with Theo Savas, please,' she said quietly to the receptionist.

Leah liked working on reception. She liked greeting people with a smile and being able to help them with their enquiries or to help them find the person they'd come to visit. This woman didn't look as though she enjoyed her job. There was no welcoming smile.

'Is he expecting you?'

'No, but I need to—'

'Mr Savas has no immediate plans to visit the London office at this time,' the receptionist informed her with precise finality.

'If I could just get a phone number—'

'I'm not authorised to give his private number out.'

'I understand, but if I could leave my number…' Leah was shaking with humiliation and embarrassment at the lack of courteous help.

The woman typed something on her screen. 'Your name and number?'

'Leah Turner,' she mumbled and then gave her phone number. 'You'll make sure he gets that message?'

'Certainly,' the woman answered with frosty dismissiveness. 'Was there anything else?'

'No. Thank you.'

It was too awful.

Leah watched her phone for days. But there was no call, no message and she could think of no other way to get in contact with him. She couldn't phone or email or scrape together the money to get to Athens…and even if she did get there, it wasn't as if she could knock on his door because she had no idea where he lived. And doubtless he'd have security staff there too—protecting him from random women.

She sighed. As much as she dreaded it, she was going to have to go back to his wretched bank.

CHAPTER FOUR

'DO YOU HAVE a moment, Theo?'

Theo glanced up as his security chief, Philip, paused in his doorway, an ominous-looking red file in his hands.

'Of course.' Theo sat back in his chair, eyes narrowing as Philip entered and closed the door behind him. 'What is it?'

'A woman visited the London office last week,' Philip said without preamble. 'The guard on the ground noticed her before she went up to Reception. There was also a call to the Greek office the day before.'

A woman? Theo raised his brows at Philip's ferociously serious expression. 'You think she's a threat?'

Philip extracted a photo from the folder. 'We pulled this from the security footage. It's the woman you asked for that summary report on a few months ago. Leah Turner.'

Theo stilled as every muscle in his body tensed. Leah? His Leah-of-the-Lost-Ticket?

He stared at the glossy image Philip had put on his desk and tried to breathe but it was as if a monster had grabbed his guts in a giant fist and squeezed hard. Because it was her—all legs and pale skin. In this picture she wore a wool jacket and a worried look. Why?

'What did she want?' His voice was so gravelly he barely recognised it as his own.

'To speak with you on a personal matter.'

She'd tried to contact him? Why now? Why months later? A surge of triumph ripped through him, swiftly followed by anger. 'Why wasn't she put through?'

He sighed and held up his hand. 'Never mind.' His staff would never interrupt him for, or give out his personal details to, a woman who'd just called in. 'Did she leave her number?'

'Unfortunately the details she left at Reception were mislaid.' Philip frowned. 'I've just interviewed the staff member—'

'How long ago was this?' Theo snapped.

'It didn't cross my desk until this morning.' Philip sounded apologetic. 'I'm sorry for the delay.'

Theo drew a steadying breath as he stared at

her picture, but it didn't stop the roar of his blood as feral *want* blazed. But that want mixed with a deeper delight. He'd *missed* her. A flat-out desperate need to know ached.

'Would you like me to—?'

'Leave it with me,' Theo dismissed him brusquely, needing privacy to process. 'And close the door on your way out.'

He needed to be alone to breathe and think and dampen down the fire arcing through his body.

'Philip,' he relented just as his man reached the door. 'Thank you.'

He hadn't opened the report on the lovely Leah Turner. He'd ordered it after that night they'd shared because he'd found himself unable to stop thinking about her. He'd half hoped to discover something in the report that would kill his constant interest in her. But it had got so bad that when the report had arrived he'd decided to exercise restraint and not even read the thing—to prove his self-control to himself and not make that intolerable yearning worse. Usually he was very good at self-control. So that report sat in a file on his home screen. Mocking him. Tempting him.

Every night since the ballet, he'd dreamed of being with her again and again. His imagination had inevitably returned to her dark hair, her pale skin, her long, long limbs... But it was the loss of something more ephemeral that had kept him awake—the sparkle in her eyes when she'd made one of her surprisingly astute comments or inadvertent slips of the tongue, the shy playfulness that had emerged with only a little encouragement and most of all that soft laugh and the emotional expressiveness that he'd found both a welcome and a warning...the thing he'd been most unable to resist responding to.

She'd not wanted to see him again. She'd not wanted his number. She'd avoided his touch in the morning. He'd taken that to be a kind of self-preservation instinct, because he too knew finality was for the best.

Circumstance had then buried Theo in a gamut of responsibility. On his return to Athens that day, Dimitri had taken a turn for the worse, forcing Theo to cancel all upcoming travel. For months he'd stayed home to oversee Dimitri's care while working around the clock to keep the business on track. The old man was finally better now and he'd even revived that inconvenient idea to find Theo a suitable wife. But, for all his comments to placate Dimitri, Theo still had zero intention of following through on the idea.

Now he stared at the still of Leah—wrapped in that bulky wool jacket despite the spring weather—and it was her worried expression that struck him most. Why had she wanted to see him? Why now—all these months later?

He shoved his chair back and stood, rapidly assessing the pros and cons of immediate departure. But the decision was already made. He needed to see her in person.

He'd needed that for months.

CHAPTER FIVE

THE IMPERIOUS KNOCKING on her door startled Leah so much she dropped a stitch. She scrambled to her feet, heart thudding as she crossed the room. She didn't get visitors at this time of night.

'Hello?' she called through her door.

'Open up, Leah.'

Her knees actually buckled. She braced both hands on the door—whether to keep herself upright or hold the door secure she wasn't sure, as raw elation flared a split second before fear exploded. A welter of emotions cascaded through her body. Was that really—?

'Leah? It's Theo.'

He was so arrogant he didn't give his surname. He didn't need to.

'Open up, Leah.'

She was so thrown she obeyed almost without thinking, somehow distanced from reality. She saw dark blue jeans first, and then glanced up to take in the white tee stretched snug across a masculine chest that looked so powerful a rush of something illicit pooled low in her belly. She snapped her attention further north, only to be ensnared by his gorgeously rare green gaze.

Time simply stopped.

She had to tell him.

'Theo.' She dragged in a decent breath, trying to clear her head.

The casual clothing didn't make him any less powerful or less intimidating than when he'd been in his perfect suit. If anything he seemed more dangerous. He looked literally edgier, as if a little loss of weight had sharpened his features, making them more starkly apparent. He was more sensational than she remembered. Her body hummed and all she wanted was to move closer.

'What are you doing here?' she asked vacantly, still unable to stop staring.

He didn't answer. He was too busy staring back at her. His gaze trawled over every inch of her face, then her body. Her self-consciousness grew as the silence thickened. Her leggings were so faded they were more grey than black, with a hole at the knee, and her oldest pair of lurid leg warmers were barely clutching her calves. Her tee was old too. But happily it was loose. She curled her toes into the thin rug beneath her feet, almost squirming through his undeniably sensual inspection. Everything—her thoughts, senses, wants—heightened. It was as if she'd only been half alive these last few months and the second he'd crossed her threshold she'd been plugged back into the mains power supply. Energy and excitement thrummed through her veins.

She had to tell him.

'I heard you were trying to get in touch with me.' He smiled but his eyes were sharp as he watched her jerkily step away from him.

She couldn't smile back. She wasn't sure she could even speak. But now was the time. Horribly short of breath but trying to hide it, she leaned against the wall for support as he closed her door and walked into the middle of her too-small flat.

'How did you hear that?' she asked.

'You called into the London branch.'

'So you got my message.'

'Unfortunately the message was lost or I'd have got here sooner.'

He hadn't got the message? 'If you didn't get the message then how—?'

'There were cameras, security guards.'

'And I looked suspicious?' She'd laugh if she

weren't so terrified about telling him. 'How did you get my address?'

'My security team is very good.'

At what? Protecting him from the unwanted attentions of women? Did they have to do that often?

His gaze didn't waver from her. 'All of this is irrelevant. Why did you want to see me, Leah?'

She felt as if she were standing on the edge of a very high precipice and had no choice but to jump off. 'I'm pregnant.'

He didn't move. In fact he remained so still she wondered if she'd actually said it. Had her words even been audible? She swallowed hard.

'I'm pregnant.' She made herself repeat it, only now her throat had tightened so much it came out on a husky breath.

'Congratulations,' he said mechanically.

She stared, waiting for more of a response. But he still didn't move. She realised he didn't fully understand. She made herself breathe again and pushed on. 'I'm pregnant by you.'

'No.' He was uncompromising in stance and in denial. 'It's not mine. We slept together months ago.'

'Yes. I'm four months pregnant.'

His mouth compressed and his searing gaze

skimmed over her body again. 'You don't look four months pregnant. You'd be larger.'

'And you're an expert?' Anger suddenly bubbled within her—she wasn't an idiot and she wasn't going to let him treat her like one. 'Because I'm so tall, there's room for the baby to hide,' she muttered. 'But the doctor said everything's developing okay.'

He stared at her fixedly. 'It's not possible. I used condoms.'

'Well, apparently one of them failed.' Her heart clogged her throat, choking her.

He remained rigid in the centre of the small room. 'And you've known all this time?'

'No, of course not.' She frowned. 'I only found out last week.'

An almost vicious brightness lit his eyes, slicing through her. 'Well, I'm no expert,' he drawled, 'but how is *that* possible?'

'I…um…' She swallowed. 'I've been so busy, I just didn't realise—'

'You didn't realise?' He stepped forward before stopping himself with a jerk. Tension streamed from his body.

She winced at the flare of fury in his eyes. 'I went to the doctor last week. She confirmed it. Then I tried to contact you.'

'You tried?' he echoed sarcastically.

A horrible hot feeling slithered inside as she nodded.

'You phoned my office but didn't leave your number. You walked into the London office once. You gave up pretty quickly.'

His scathing assessment flayed. He was right. She'd not done enough.

He shook his head. 'Am I the only possible father?'

His question stabbed—how could he think otherwise? She paused; had he had other lovers since her? Of course, he probably had. That reality hurt more than it should. But he'd known she'd been a virgin—hadn't he realised how rare it was for her?

'You think I started having casual sex every other night?' She glared at him. 'We can get a DNA test if you don't believe me.'

His eyes blazed before he abruptly turned away, rolling his shoulders. 'No. It's okay. I believe you.' His voice sounded flat and hard. He drew in a deep breath and swung back to face her. 'What's the plan?'

'Plan?' she echoed.

'You're four months pregnant. You'd failed to contact me, so what were you going to do?'

'I was going to…' She swallowed. She'd been trying to get over her panic enough to make progress. She'd been failing on that so far.

'Were you going to go home to your parents?' He watched her closely.

'No,' she muttered. She wasn't ready to face the recriminations and rolled eyes, the sighs of impatience because she'd failed to meet their standards again. She couldn't even move to another city and make a success of it.

'You haven't told them either?'

'They're very busy and they live too far away.' She'd never want her baby in that cold intellectual environment where normal people couldn't perform highly enough.

'I live even further away.' He stepped towards her. 'Have you thought about that?'

She hadn't thought about it at all. She'd not been able to get past worrying about telling him. Frankly she'd been too paralysed to predict his reaction. But it was bad. Bitter betrayal burned in his eyes and he was coldly furious, the antithesis of the man she'd trusted so completely that night. There was no softening in his reserve now.

'You travel a lot.' She tried to reason a way out of the mess. 'If you want, you can visit…a lot.'

'If I want?' He looked astounded. 'You think

I'll settle for seeing my child every other week at best?' The lethal way he fired his words made goosebumps lift—let alone the impact of what he'd actually said.

He loomed closer, even angrier. 'Not going to happen, Leah. *Never* going to happen. Have you talked to *anyone* about this?'

'Only the doctor.' She hated how pathetically breathy her answer sounded.

She'd not told anyone at work. She'd avoided Maeve. She'd not returned Zoe's last call… She'd been in denial.

'Good. That means we can work out our story more effectively.'

'Our story?'

'We're getting married.'

'What?' Her jaw dropped.

'You're pregnant. It's my baby. I'm not having my child born illegitimate.'

'And I don't get any choice in this?'

'So explain your choice to me, then. What are you going to do? Stay in this tiny bedsit? Are you going to head straight back to work the second you've given birth and leave my baby in a nursery all day? How did you think you were going to make ends meet, Leah?'

He was asking too many questions. Making

too many judgments. A barrage of tests designed to trip her up—like those dreaded pop quizzes her parents inflicted on her randomly and repeatedly so she never had any chance of relaxing. Not when she failed them every time because their required pass mark was one hundred per cent correct. That old performance anxiety reared, rendering her unable to think at all. Instead she lashed out. 'I'm *not* going to marry you.'

'Why not? You know you'll never have to work another day in your life,' he exploded.

As if that were relevant? 'I didn't even know who you were. I wasn't the one who provided the condoms. Or the one who put them on. I'm not the one who didn't bother to check they'd…' She trailed off.

'Survived the event?' he interpolated with dry precision.

'No. And guess what? I like my life. I like my home here. I like the people I help in my job. I want to work. I certainly don't want to leave it all to live a life of intolerable boredom in a foreign country with a husband who resents me.'

His face whitened. 'Too bad,' he choked. 'Because here we are. It isn't what you want? It's not what I want either. But it's what's *right*. Pack your things.'

She stared at the stranger he'd become. Or perhaps he always was this ruthless and she'd just not seen it that night because she'd stupidly given him everything he'd wanted? She couldn't reconcile that suave, amusing man with the cold authoritarian before her now.

'I don't want to fight, Leah.' He ran a hand through his hair roughly.

'You just want me to do everything you want.'

'Yeah.' He actually threw a smile in her direction. Well, a tight, determined baring of the teeth that a more generous person might mistake for a smile. 'I'm good at fixing problems and you have to agree this is a problem.'

It was a huge problem. 'What's your plan, then?'

He ruffled his hair again and then sighed. 'In the long term, we won't have to impact on each other's lives much.'

Chills swept over her skin. This was no romance. No rescue. He wasn't suggesting marriage because he *liked* her. This was only about securing their child's future. But the details were too scarce. 'What do you mean?'

'I mean we can come up with an arrangement that suits us both.'

Still not enough. 'What kind of arrangement?'

He had a distant look in his eyes. 'We'll marry, we'll raise this child. But you and I will live largely separate lives. I have several properties.'

'Separate.' She swallowed the sting of his cool rejection. She couldn't let it bother her. He clearly didn't feel any of the attraction to her that she still felt for him. Not even just physical. 'Theo, we had a really nice night, but it was supposed to end there,' she said stoutly.

'Well, there's no ending it now,' he muttered. 'We're stuck with each other for a lifetime.'

'We don't have to be.'

'What does that mean?' he asked pointedly. 'Are you prepared to give me full custody?'

All the air whooshed from her lungs. 'What? No!'

'Because I'll not step back from my responsibility, Leah. If you're having my baby, I'm going to provide for it. Always.'

His vehemence shocked her. He'd said he didn't want to marry. She'd thought that meant he'd not want children either…but now he was all 'instant family'—why?

'Don't make this more difficult than it needs to be,' he added, watching her closely, his expression shutting down as if he could read the questions burning inside her. 'We can work it out.'

'Yes,' she agreed. 'But it doesn't have to mean marriage.' She struggled to drag in a calming breath. 'You said you'd never marry.'

Theo's jaw locked so hard it hurt. 'You're pregnant.'

Nothing but regret filled him. History was repeating in the worst of ways. He'd failed her, his grandfather, himself. He knew accidents happened. He was one himself. And he had to do a better job of fixing this than his parents had. And as much as he didn't want it, there was only one way to do that. But he could hardly compute what she'd told him. Truthfully he was still recovering from being in the same airspace as her again—still battling the urge to haul her close and kiss her. He needed calm and logic to create a cool-headed contract with her.

Yet as he stared, as she stiffened in defensiveness, a primal possessiveness stole his reason, its fierceness shocking his self-control from him. He'd claim what was his. He'd *protect* it. Always. He'd even protect it from himself.

'I won't have an illegitimate child, Leah,' he

said roughly. 'He or she deserves my name and all the privileges that come with it.'

'You mean money?'

'I mean many things, but, yes, that's one of them. My child also needs the proper protection... You do too.' He glanced at her. 'You have no idea what comes with wealth like ours.'

'Is it a terrible burden?' Her eyes glinted as she lobbed the acerbic little taunt.

He refused to react to her bite. 'The child also needs more than physical security. A sense of belonging.' Theo closed his mind to his own old memories of insecurity and betrayal. 'I'm sorry if that's too old-fashioned for you, but...' Bitterness almost overwhelmed him. Surely he could give more than he'd received? Except he really couldn't bear the thought of caring for a tiny, vulnerable baby. He didn't have what it took.

'It's not old-fashioned. It's honourable.' She sighed. 'It's just—'

'We're talking about a baby, Leah,' he interrupted, unable to stand the argument, let alone the actual reality. 'It doesn't get more life-changing than that. I'll take my share of the responsibility.'

Her lips compressed. 'But you're taking *all*

the responsibility and becoming a dictator in the process.'

Her flash of temper tested his determination not to lose his again. But if he reacted now the way he really wanted, then this wouldn't become the safe, serviceable arrangement they both needed. Her earlier words haunted him—*a life of intolerable boredom with a husband who resented her*? She'd encapsulated his mother's life in one sentence. And look at the mess of betrayal and hurt that had led to.

He refused to excavate the past now. All that mattered was that he ensured Leah had everything she needed. Except he didn't really know how—not beyond the basics of providing four walls, a roof and food. He paced across the tiny room, rapidly working out the only way they could forge a viable future. She'd hardly have to see him. They simply had to agree to the arrangement.

Right now she wouldn't look at him. She was scared and angry. Frankly so was he. 'Pack your things. It's getting late.'

She kept staring at the floor. 'I'm not leaving with you.'

'I'm not leaving without you.' Her persistence tore his temper. 'You might have only recently found out about this pregnancy, but you didn't exactly try hard to get in touch with me. How do I know you're not going to skip town in the middle of the night?'

'You don't trust me.'

He braced inwardly at the hurt he heard in that soft sentence and just reiterated the fact. 'I'm not leaving without you.'

'Well, I'm not leaving here tonight. Good luck on my tiny sofa.'

'I'm not sleeping on the sofa, Leah.'

'You're not welcome in my bed,' she declared huskily.

'Is that right?' He stepped closer and felt the frisson of sensual awareness. Her words were pure challenge—a denial of the electricity sparking between them. It was still there—he'd seen it the second they'd laid eyes on each other again. But it was in both their interests to let her deny it. 'Then it's my hotel suite.'

'I'm not—'

'It has more than one bedroom,' he growled. 'Will that appease your outraged virtue?' He whirled away so he wasn't tempted to prove how hollow her words were. But the room wasn't anywhere near large enough for him to get the distance he needed. 'It's that or we stand here arguing all night.'

She folded her arms. 'I can't just pack up everything tonight.'

He glanced about. 'Why not? It won't take long.'

She shook her head. 'You're a jerk, you know that?'

'Leah.' He struggled for control—so close to throwing her over his shoulder and carting her down to the waiting car himself. He never let his emotions get the better of him, but it was almost impossible now. 'It's getting late.'

'I could join you later. In a week or so.'

It was unacceptable to him. 'We're sticking together until we're married.'

She looked aghast. 'We can't just get married.'

True. He nodded. 'It'll take about a week to get the paperwork processed.'

'A *week*?'

Yeah, he was moving fast but he'd make no apology for it. He could only try a little joke. 'That'll give you time to find something to wear.'

'Because that's the most important thing I have to consider?'

He bit back his smile as she slammed her retort at him. Backed into a corner, she could still hold her own.

'Stop stalling for time and go pack or we'll go without any of your clothes.' He was right about this. She just needed to admit it.

'Fine. Your suite. Separate rooms.' She marched all of five feet through to the bedroom.

Theo paced around the small lounge again. It was small and drab, the carpet worn and the walls in desperate need of a fresh lick of paint. But he noticed the few decorations she'd added to personalise the place—the warm-looking throws draped over the sofa, the knitted cushion covers. Then he spotted the pinboard. There was a photo of Leah with that ballet friend of hers, the menu of a Thai take-away around the corner, a couple of hand-drawn designs on grid paper, a theatre ticket. He peered closer.

'This is your ticket to the ballet?' he asked as she returned with a rucksack and that ginormous ugly handbag.

A rush of memory loosened his restraint and he smiled.

'It turns out I'd left it here all along.' She looked embarrassed. 'That night, that's why I couldn't find it in my bag. Pretty useless, I know.' She actually smiled.

He couldn't hold back his little laugh and studied the ticket again. 'You had quite a good seat.'

'I told you, Zoe is my friend.' She glanced at him. 'Or do you not believe me about that now?' Soft hurt flickered in her eyes, fading out that smile. 'I've never given you reason *not* to trust me, Theo.'

She didn't realise that, for him, trust wasn't freely given and then lost. It had to be earned. 'I guess we don't know each other very well, Leah.'

Her expression became a little pinched. 'I guess getting married will change that.'

Leah swallowed hard when he didn't reply. She'd thought she had known him. That they'd connected more than physically that night. And *she* had most certainly trusted him. For him not to trust her hurt. Now she was mortified he'd seen she'd kept that ballet ticket as a keepsake of the night they'd spent together.

She picked up her rucksack again. 'I'll need to come back to get everything else.'

As wary as she was of going with him, how could she argue? He was right—what alternative could she suggest? She didn't have his kind of money, power, experience or authority. And not only would her family be mortified and unwilling to help, they were actually *unable* to offer the emotional support she really wanted for her child. If Theo had a warm relationship with his grandfather, and he seemed to, then that might be better. At the very least she had to give him the chance. She owed him that.

'You have a current passport?' he checked.

'Yes. Why?'

'Because we need to get home quickly.'

'You expect me to go to *Greece*? When? To-morrow?'

'Exactly.'

It was happening too fast. Get married in a week? Go to Greece tomorrow? Leave with him tonight?

He watched her solemnly. 'We need to work this out and I can't leave my family for long.'

'But you think I can leave mine?'

'You haven't told your parents the good news. I guess that says a lot about your relationship with them.' He took the bags from her. 'We'll fly to Athens first thing in the morning.'

'I can't just not turn up to my work.' She couldn't believe his arrogance. 'I need to work out my notice. I need to say goodbye to my residents. Or do you think that because I'm just a receptionist I can ditch everything and leap to your beck and call?'

He stared at her fixedly, rather as if he was inwardly counting to ten. 'Okay.' He released a slow sigh. 'We'll figure it out in the morning. For now, let's get to my hotel and get some rest.'

Leah stared stonily out of the passenger window at the darkening sky and said nothing. It wasn't the same hotel as that night at the ballet. This one was polite discretion with no big logos—secret luxury in the heart of Mayfair. She followed Theo to the suite on the top floor. The lounge alone was almost three times the size of her little flat.

'Take whichever room you want,' he muttered.

'You've not taken one already?'

'I came straight from the airport to your apartment.'

The atmosphere thickened. He'd not known her news but he'd come straight to see her? Just because she'd appeared in his London office?

She couldn't turn away from his gaze. It was as if she were pinned in place by that intense scrutiny. Somehow this place felt more intimate than her apartment despite it being so much bigger. Maybe it was the mood lighting or the luxuriousness of the furnishings, but suddenly she was too aware of sensation, the temptation of intimacy and touch. Smoky memories curled. She gritted her teeth, wanting to regain control of herself. He didn't want *that*. He wanted them to live separate lives, together in name only for the sake of their baby.

'I'll come with you to talk to your boss tomorrow before we leave for the airport,' he said huskily.

'Because I'm incapable of talking to them on my own?' She couldn't hold back her defensiveness. 'Are you afraid I'll say something I shouldn't?'

'No.' He stepped closer. 'Because I'm afraid they won't let you go. One of those oldies will ask you to make them a pot of tea and we'll never get you out of there.' He gazed at her intently. 'You're a pushover, Leah. A tug on the heartstrings is all it takes.'

A tug on the heartstrings? Was that what he'd done with her that night? Had that connection she'd thought they'd forged just been a ploy? She shook her head, not able to believe that. 'There's nothing wrong with being kind to people.'

'Nothing at all.' He gazed at her for another moment, then rolled his shoulders. 'We'll go see your parents after we've been to your work in the morning. What are they like?'

'You don't need to—' She couldn't tell him about her parents and she certainly didn't want him to meet them. 'Just forget I mentioned it. I don't need to go see them.'

'You're going to leave the country and not even see them to say goodbye? You don't want to invite them to the wedding?'

'They won't come.'

He blinked. 'Now I can't wait to meet them.'

'Too bad,' she echoed his earlier dismissal. 'You're not.'

'Leah,' he sighed. 'I'm trying to meet you half-way. I'm trying *not* to be a dictator.'

'So by simply informing me of tomorrow's itinerary, you're *not* being a dictator?' she asked.

He took her shoulders in a firm grip. 'I'm going to be their son-in-law, you don't think they'd want to meet me—vet me first?' A quizzical look lit his eyes. 'There's no need for me to pass any parental approval?'

They'd probably love to meet him. But they wouldn't believe for a second that he was in love with her. They'd see the situation for what it was—a hoax. A mortifying necessity because she'd stuffed up. For them to know that? She wanted to shrivel into a ball and hide. She didn't need them to witness yet another of her failures. Because they expected nothing less, right?

'Tell me about them.' He cocked his head, watching her as if he were trying to solve a cryptic puzzle. 'What do they do? It can't be that bad.'

'It's not that I'm ashamed of them, more the other way round.' She huffed a sigh. 'They're academics. My younger brother too. They've lived near the university all my life.'

'Academics?' His eyebrows lifted.

'Professors, in fact. And my younger brother, Oliver, is so gifted he's already a senior lecturer.' While she was a receptionist at a care home. 'Their careers are everything to them.'

He looked thoughtful. 'What do they think of your career choice?'

'You mean you can't guess?'

He gave her shoulders a gentle squeeze. 'What's their specialisation?'

'Other than criticism?' she half joked. 'Chemistry.'

'Chemistry?' His eyes widened and he couldn't suppress his smile.

She couldn't resist a small smile back, but then she had a flash of how awkward it was going to be. 'My parents are very—' She broke off, unable to explain just how laser-precise their perceptions were. 'They'll see in a second that we're not...'

'Not what?' He waited. 'You're having my baby so we've obviously had sex. We find each other attractive.'

'We *found* each other attractive. *Once.*'

That intensity deepened in his expression. His vivid green eyes were backlit with remnants of that magic night and the phantom delight he'd showered upon her. 'I thought you always opted for the truth, Leah,' he said quietly.

'Well.' She sucked in a steadying breath. 'Maybe you were right. Sometimes it might be better not to say anything.'

'Denial?' His smile faded as he gazed down at her. 'For protection.'

That heat spiralled like a whisper of smoke within her. More memories teased—of sizzling touch and sweet torment. But she had to ignore the urge to lean closer, and pull back instead. Because he didn't want her. He wanted separate lives.

'It's late,' she muttered. 'I should get some rest.'

'Yes. Go. Sleep.' He released her, that remote, reserved man once more. 'It seems we have a big day tomorrow.'

CHAPTER SIX

'OF COURSE, YOU must leave right away, Leah,' Seth said quietly. 'But we're really going to miss you.'

Leah nodded; her throat had tightened too much to answer.

Her boss sent her a smile that was both encouraging and sad before he turned to Theo. 'There really was no need for you to give us such a generous donation…'

'Leah was concerned about leaving you so quickly without a replacement organised,' Theo said. 'But with my grandfather the way he is…'

'Of course. We understand.' Seth glanced back to Leah. 'But we are sad to see you go.'

Leah looked to the floor to hide her emotion. This was the first job she'd loved and the first job she'd totally nailed. There'd been no massive list of qualifications required, just the ability to put people at ease. Her life had blossomed here—she was going to miss it too.

'I need a quick moment,' she murmured to Theo and walked down the corridor before he had a chance to respond.

She stopped at Maeve's open door and lightly rapped her fingers on the frame.

'You're leaving us.' Maeve pushed out of her plush armchair and held her arms out.

'Yes.' Leah stepped in and gave the tiny woman a tight hug. 'But I have something I wanted to give you.' She stepped back, blinking quickly and pulling out the small knee blanket she'd put in her handbag.

'It's the purple, with that rib I can't manage with my arthritic old hands.' Maeve took it from her with a smile.

'Yes.' Leah smiled past the lump in her throat. 'I thought it would help keep those draughts out.' Maeve couldn't knit the complex patterns she used to, and Leah knew she felt the cold.

'I have something for you too.' Maeve picked up a clear bag from her table and held it out to Leah. 'I decided on white, seeing you weren't sure...'

Leah's heart melted as she lifted out a tiny woollen baby jacket. 'Maeve, it's just beautiful. Thank you so much.' Her throat closed. It would have taken a lot of effort for Maeve to get it finished in time and Leah would treasure it always.

Maeve clasped Leah's fingers with her shaking hands. 'You're going to be a wonderful mother, Leah.'

Leah blinked, warmth flooding her. This relationship was so precious to her. 'I'll come and visit you when I'm in town again.' Her throat tightened. She didn't want to say goodbye. She was going to miss her. She was going to miss all the people she'd been working with.

'Leah,' Theo called quietly from the doorway. 'I'm sorry. We need to go.'

'Is that him?' Maeve asked.

'Yes.' Leah half chuckled as she saw the shrewd assessment in Maeve's eyes as she craned her neck to take stock of Theo.

'You'll take care of her, won't you?' Maeve questioned him pointedly.

As embarrassed as she was, warm amusement and appreciation trickled through Leah. It touched her that Maeve cared. She cared about her too.

Theo smiled his most charming smile. 'Yes.'

Ten minutes later Leah stared out of the window as the car sped out of central London, her pulse accelerating at the same pace. The driver had closed the partition, giving them a level of privacy she didn't really want. When she was alone with Theo, her thoughts went a little wild.

'I can't believe you used your money and your grandfather to get me out of my contract,' she muttered.

'I wasn't using my grandfather. I told the truth,' Theo answered calmly.

'Well, you certainly used your money,' she murmured, submitting to the niggling need to provoke him.

'Leah.' He reached out and covered her clenched fist with his hand.

His touch stilled her antagonism but she couldn't rid herself of all her anxiety. She knew they would resolve this situation and, while he was annoyingly decisive, he was at least trying. She should do the same.

'Your grandfather is really that unwell?' she asked.

'He had heart surgery recently.' Theo's tone grew reserved. 'But he's getting better.'

She wondered why he was reticent about him. 'How's he going to feel about this?'

His expression hardened and he released her hand. 'It'll be fine.'

Leah watched him closely. 'He's just going to

be okay with you turning up engaged to a woman you barely know, who's four months along already?'

'Dimitri doesn't need to know every detail—or lack thereof—of our relationship.'

'You're going to lie to him?'

'I'll tell him the important facts and that's enough. His well-being is paramount.'

Would he be upset by some of the 'less important' facts?

She paused, sensing his reluctance to talk, but she was unable to resist probing further. He'd asked about her family—couldn't she do the same? 'You're close?'

His hesitation made her senses even more acute.

'I've lived with him since I was ten.' His voice was so low it was hard to hear over the purr of the engine. 'I owe him everything.'

'Why did you go to live with him?'

'My father passed away.'

'I'm sorry.' She gazed at him. His emotionless countenance was unsettling.

'I went to live with Dimitri. That is why I'm not going to abandon my child now.' He drew in a sharp breath. 'We can do better...'

Because *he'd* felt abandoned? Leah swallowed

back the deeply personal questions that sprang to mind. He'd not mentioned his mother and she was wary of asking more because there was pain in his expressionlessness. Her heart ached as her apprehension rose. 'What's your grandfather—Dimitri—like?'

He sighed, but the faintest smile softened his mouth. 'Authoritarian, old and unwell. I won't let him be upset by anything or anyone.'

'Do you think he'll be upset by me?' She bit her lip, anxious about the answer.

He glanced at her, his eyes flaring with something before his lashes lowered. 'No one could be upset by you.'

Somehow it wasn't the answer she'd wanted. Somehow it skittled the little emotional self-control she'd restored. 'Because I'm just a harmless little thing who couldn't possibly hurt anyone?' she asked.

Because she was powerless and inconsequential? As useless as her parents had made her feel? The parents she was about to face and confess her life-changing mistake to?

'Because you're a kind person who'd never be deliberately rude to anyone.' He held her gaze solemnly. 'But you shouldn't have to put up with him either. You won't see him much.'

She blinked. 'I don't have to put up with him? Is he scary?'

'He used to be.' A whisker of a smile flashed on his face. 'But then I grew up. He only wants what he thinks is best for me.'

'He was tough on you when you were younger?'

Another hesitation made her lean closer to listen.

'He had exacting standards and I needed to prove myself to him. But I'm grateful for them. We get on well. As I said, I owe him everything.'

Leah knew all about exacting standards but, unlike her, Theo would have surpassed them all.

The car ate up the miles to Cambridge and her nerves ratcheted. The research institute was so familiar—the white walls and bright lights beneath which she'd faded, invisible and insignificant. She'd eventually realised that restocking the chemicals cupboard wasn't the job for her. She needed a job where she was around people more. And she'd needed to get away from the triple eclipse of her family.

Drawing a deep breath, she knocked on the door of her parents' office. They'd both be there. They always were.

'Leah?' Her father looked up from his desk. 'This is a surprise. Is everything all right?'

Of course he'd immediately assume things might not be all right. Leah tried not to let that bitterness rise. It wasn't their fault that, for super-smart people, they couldn't understand her.

'Everything is...' she drew breath '...really great. Is Mum here too?'

'Of course.' It was her mother who replied.

Leah took satisfaction at the swiftly concealed surprise on Theo's face as her mother appeared from the next room. While her father was like her—tall, thin and dark-haired—her mother was the absolute opposite. Short, blonde, beautiful and brilliant enough to earn her double PhD in half the time it normally took, Leah's mum adored challenging stereotypes—insisting women didn't need to meet societal expectations of beauty or brilliance. She'd rejected make-up, dresses, high heels and insisted Leah never wear them either. Only her mother wasn't angular and un-pretty like Leah—she had no idea what it was like not to be wildly attractive naturally.

'What brings you here?' Her mother looked at her. 'And your friend?'

'This is Theo Savas,' Leah began. 'Theo, these are my parents, Jocelyn Franks and James Turner.' Her nerves tightened.

Theo extended a hand. For a moment her father

just stared at it before giving it a weak response. She should have told Theo her parents weren't physically demonstrative people.

'We're here because…um…actually, you're going to be grandparents.' She just blurted it out.

'Pardon?' Anger—and that old impatience—built on her mother's face, mottling her flawless skin.

'I'm pregnant.' Leah tried to stay calm but her brain was malfunctioning the way it always did when her mother was about to test her on one of her many impossible quizzes.

'You're responsible for this?' Her mother turned to Theo. 'Did you take advantage of her?'

Leah gaped. Couldn't *she* be responsible? Was she invisible all over again? She refused to be that—not in front of Theo. Not when she now knew some people believed in her. People like Seth and Maeve. 'Maybe I took advantage of him?'

'Oh, Leah.'

That withering dismissal, that disappointment?

Leah pasted on her smile, determined not to let this happen in front of Theo. 'We're getting married in Greece next week—'

'I should think so.' Her father turned with low fury to Theo. 'You're going to take care of her?'

It was the same question Maeve had asked but it sprang from something so different. He wasn't asking Theo this because he thought she was a treasure, worthy of only the best treatment. But because he thought she was the opposite—helpless and hopeless.

'I knew it was a mistake to let you go to London on your own—'

'I might not have your PhDs, but I'm not stupid—'

'You've just told us you're *pregnant*.'

'And that makes me stupid?' She gazed at her mother sadly. Because having a child was a bad thing? That was her mother's attitude, wasn't it? Or, at least, having a child who was an eternal disappointment was.

'You've got no qualifications, Leah.' Her mother shredded her. 'We've been looking after you for years, since you dropped out. We got you that job in the lab—'

'I've been looking after you,' Leah pointed out in a choked voice. 'Who cooked all the meals? Who arranged everything you were too busy for?'

'That was to give you something to do.' Her mother glared at her. 'You think we can't cook, Leah?'

'You never did.'

'You know it's not the best use of our time,' her father said.

Leah gaped. Because her parents' time was more precious than hers? Their 'real' work—all those intellectual achievements—were too important to be interrupted with anything like parenting or maintaining a normal house? They'd paid for a cleaner and now it seemed they'd just 'allowed' Leah to do the cooking. How marvellously kind of them. Hadn't they thought she might have plans and dreams of her own that she'd rather be fulfilling?

She'd realised how desperately she'd needed to start over and live her own life. And she'd been succeeding. And she'd continue to succeed without them.

'Well.' She cleared her throat. 'Thanks for keeping an eye out for me all this time but you no longer need trouble yourselves. We're leaving for Greece today.'

'Leah.' Her father frowned, his tone patronising. 'You can't just—'

'I'm sorry if you can't make it to the wedding, given it's such short notice.' Theo stepped forward. 'But we can't delay our happy occasion a day longer than necessary.' He wrapped his arm around her and drew her too close. 'Leah is so special to me. I'll take care of her and our baby.' He gazed into her eyes as if he were love-struck. 'You don't need to worry about her.'

She wanted to point out that she didn't need *any* of them to 'take care of her'. But there was a glimmer of something more than amusement in his expression and it hurt. She didn't want his sympathy. But as he looked at her that expression deepened to devastatingly serious. 'Anyway, you've never needed to worry about her. She can look after herself—'

'Leah? I didn't know you were here for a visit.'

She turned, pulling out of Theo's hold as her brother, Oliver, walked into the office.

'I'm just leaving.' She braced because her emotions were almost beyond control and she'd not expected Oliver to be away from his lab. 'I'm moving to Greece. Getting married. Having a baby. You should come to the wedding,' she summarised as swiftly as she could. 'No joke.'

'What?' Oliver pulled the beanie off and gaped at her. 'When? I have my—'

'Research, I know. It's okay. I'll send you a photo.' She just wanted to get out of there as quickly as possible because she loved her little brother. 'We need to leave now.'

She walked, not even checking to see if Theo was with her. She knew he would be. Just as she knew her parents wouldn't stop her. But as she crossed the threshold her brother called her name. She couldn't not glance back.

'You'll phone?' He was still gaping.

'Of course.' Because she knew he couldn't say it as well, but he did care.

He saluted her and realised he held the beanie. He suddenly smiled. 'Thanks for this. It's the best one yet.'

She nodded and left. She was going to miss Oliver the most—she'd cared for her younger brother, even when he'd been too buried in books to realise he needed it.

She couldn't trust herself to speak as they got back into the car. Theo apparently had a few things to digest too, because the first fifteen minutes of the drive back were in complete silence. But then she felt him turn towards her.

'Your family are—'

'Amazing, I know.' She smiled brightly because it was that or burst into tears.

'That wasn't the word I was going to use.'

'But they are,' she argued lightly. 'Bona fide geniuses, the three of them. With just a normal IQ, I'm the odd one out.' She shook her head but was unable to stop the words tumbling. 'You didn't need to step in. You didn't need to act as if…'

'As if what?' His eyes glinted. 'I actually *want* to marry you?'

'I don't need you to say that to them. Or take care of me now.' She couldn't hold back. Her parents' words had stung. Just because she didn't have three degrees didn't mean she was incapable of looking after herself. 'I'm not incompetent. I could have made it work. Women do, you know, raise kids on their own.'

He reached out and covered her tight fist with his big hand. 'I know you could handle this alone, Leah. You're amazing. You just handled the hell out of *them*,' he added. 'But the point is you don't have to be alone now. You're not solely responsible for this situation.'

She desperately wished she could escape the emotion overwhelming her at his words.

'Why does your brother wear a beanie in summer?' he asked with a wry smile.

She shot him a sideways look, startled by the change in topic. 'He gets cold in the lab. And he has sensitive ears and it's better if they're warm.'

'So you gave it to him?'

'Knitting is the new black, didn't you know?'

'You made it?'

'Yes, I made it. You don't think I'm capable of that?'

'Easy, tiger.' He laughed gently. 'I'm not like them, Leah. I thought you'd bought it for him because, yes, it looked good enough quality to have been bought. You gave that little rug to that old lady at the home as well. But I get the impression your parents had very high standards.'

'I was never going to get the grades they expected from me.' She'd tried so very hard but they'd expected brilliance and perfection.

'That's why you stopped dancing?'

'They said it interfered with my schoolwork too much.' She shrugged in a helpless gesture. 'They couldn't understand why I wasn't like them and they tried so hard to make me like them—honestly, the books, the tests, the tutoring... And you see what they think of me now.' She looked at him. 'Only good for the cooking and cleaning, right? They actually think you took advantage of me. I must be rescued. I can't take care of myself. I must get walked all over...all because I don't have the same skill set or dreams they do.'

'It wasn't your fault you couldn't live up to

their expectations,' he said quietly. 'But you gave up your dream.'

'They wouldn't pay for my classes any more and I couldn't get my marks high enough to get them to resume them.'

'You didn't fight in other ways? Didn't clean the dance studio in exchange for free lessons?'

She gazed at him. Just like that he'd worked up an independent solution. That was what he would have done, or something else inventive to get what he wanted. She had no doubt he'd be defiant in the face of denial or rejection. That was why he was the CEO of a massively successful bank now. He'd have done anything to prove them wrong, wouldn't he? He had that kind of strength and self-belief. She didn't.

'I wanted to *please* them,' she whispered, that little truth torn from her. She'd wanted their love. She'd seen the warmth in their eyes when Oliver had done well—every time he'd surpassed her. She didn't begrudge his achievements— she'd only wanted a little of the adoration they'd shown him. 'I wanted their approval. I've always wanted that and I've never got it and I tried so hard for so long.' And now she was tired of trying to live up to everyone else's expectations. 'I couldn't do what they wanted. Then I couldn't do what *I* wanted because they stopped me. So then I grew a spine. I moved to London. I got my job.' She'd left and she'd had that magic night with Theo and things really had turned around. Her confidence had grown. She sniffed. 'But now I get to do what *you* want me to do.'

'Don't be sad,' he murmured, a sparkle lighting his eyes. 'I think you're going to like the island.'

'Island?'

'Your new home.'

'You mean Athens?'

'Athens initially.' He nodded. 'Then the island.'

An island that was different from Athens? 'But you work in Athens?' she clarified.

'Yes.'

So he'd be in Athens and she'd be on some other island? Was this what he'd meant about space—that she'd not actually live with him?

'You're sending me to my own kind of Alcatraz?'

He laughed. 'You don't want to know anything about it?'

'I don't need to. I'm sure its unspeakably beautiful. There'll be a pool and an amazing house and probably some billion-dollar view…but it's still a prison.' She couldn't get her head around it, couldn't consider it in any kind of positive light. 'What am I supposed to do all day?'

'You'll have assistants. Nannies. A cook.'

Was that what he'd meant when he'd said she didn't need to be alone now? He was going to arrange a massive coterie of staff for her? But *he* wasn't going to be there?

He leaned forward. 'Don't you want a break, Leah? You'll want for nothing—'

Except friends, or a partner, or a *lover*. She shivered. 'I spent too long buried away in a laboratory not talking to real people. I *like* people. I like meeting them, talking to them—'

'You'll have a tiny little person all of your own to take care of soon enough.'

'Who won't be able to talk back to me for months...'

'And as I said, you'll have staff.'

'Wonderful. People who are *paid* to spend time with me.'

He laughed. 'And, believe it or not, other people live on the island. Nice people.'

The prospect of being apart from *him* really wasn't what she wanted. But for him?

He sobered and a perplexed frown creased his forehead. 'The last thing I want is for you to be unhappy. I thought you'd want to live in a place where you can relax.' He shook his head. 'Just wait till you see it, Leah.'

She sat in silent contemplation. All her life she'd wanted someone to love her, just for her. And she wasn't about to get it. But she couldn't help wondering why Theo didn't want that too. Didn't he feel bereft at the prospect of an emotionless marriage? She was sure she hadn't imagined that flare of heat in his eyes when he'd seen her again. Didn't he even want to try to use that as a basis for something more? Obviously not.

Her heart sank all over again as she realised he truly didn't want any of it at all.

CHAPTER SEVEN

THEY WERE DRIVEN to the airport where a discreet crew were waiting for them. A tall, serious-looking man handed Theo a briefcase and murmured in his ear before he left to board ahead of them.

'I don't always use the private jet, but I thought we needed the privacy for this trip,' Theo explained as he led her up the staircase into the sleek jet.

Privacy? For what? Her pulse skipped.

'I don't want everyone watching us and wondering who you are.' He pulled a pale blue bag out of the briefcase and handed it to her as she sat in the wide luxurious leather armchair. 'We'll present you when we're ready.'

Present her? 'What's this?' She peered into the bag and saw a small jewel box nestled in tissue paper. A wave of cold trepidation washed over her but she was aware of him watching, so she faked calm. Her fingers trembled only the slightest as she opened the box and stared at the ring. 'Is it real?' she choked.

'Considering the price, I hope so.'

She gazed at the enormous diamond. Of course it was real. He was too rich to need to fake it. 'When did you get it?'

'I didn't. One of my assistants picked it up on the way to the airport. I apologise if you don't like it—apparently there was a limited selection.'

Massive solitaires were always in style, weren't they? The box blared the luxurious branding. But she couldn't quite believe he'd got someone else to buy it.

'Try it on and see if it fits.'

Because that was all that mattered—she didn't need to like it. It didn't mean anything. They just needed to make it fit and off they went as fiancés. She pushed the platinum band onto her cold finger. 'Lucky guess.'

He nodded and pulled a laptop from his briefcase. 'You can shop in Athens, get whatever else you need.'

'I don't need anything else.' She didn't need this giant lump of ice on her finger either.

'You're going to need a little more than the black tee shirts and trousers you've stuffed in that small bag. At some point that baby is going to make its presence known.'

'I'll get some bigger black tees and trousers when I need to,' she muttered obstinately. She did *not* want his wealth showered upon her. In fact, she wanted to take as little as possible from him—after all, he wanted little from her too.

But he'd glanced up from his laptop and now a small smile was flitting around his mouth. 'Why black?'

'Why not?'

'You make me think of a shadow…like you're trying not to stand out.'

'Women my height always stand out,' she pointed out grimly.

'For all the right reasons. You should make the most of your attributes.'

She gaped, momentarily unable to answer.

'And don't forget to get some more of those little scarlet silk things,' he murmured wickedly, and then looked back at his screen.

Leah stared hard at him for a while longer but apparently he was going to spend the rest of the flight working on his laptop. He'd just been amusing himself with a flippant moment. She shook her head. He was a conundrum—so often reserved and serious, and then there were flashes of fun and humour and, right this second, she really didn't like him for it.

As they landed hours later, a wave of nervous anticipation scurried along her veins. She'd never thought she'd visit Greece any time soon and she had to confess she was excited at the prospect of discovering its ancient culture and history, tasting the beautiful food, experiencing the lifestyle...although she rapidly discovered Theo's wasn't a normal lifestyle. It was almost obscene. She had only a moment to breathe in the warmer, vibrant atmosphere before more security guys in tailored suits and silence escorted them from the plane to a powerful black car with tinted windows. She glimpsed a bustling city filled with people, traffic, buildings, but they drove for quite a while and eventually the landscape changed. The properties became bigger with green spaces between them. Off a side street she saw palm trees forming a guard of honour the length of an esplanade.

'You live in the suburbs?' Somehow it wasn't quite what she'd expected.

'We have a compound on the coastline now known as the Athenian Rivera,' he said solemnly. 'The land has been in the family for decades.'

A compound? On a riviera? Leah had only seen such things in music videos.

'Will I meet Dimitri tonight?' she asked.

'Tomorrow would be better. He should be resting for the night by now.'

He'd gone all remote again—she felt the tension in his silence and the loss of his smile. All earlier easiness was now omitted from his demeanour. She focused on what she could see, catching glimpses of a beautiful mansion-lined beach just before they turned into a driveway. Large gates automatically swung back to allow the car through. They rounded a corner and a building came into view—not old and traditional but sleek and modern, extremely opulent and stylish. As she gaped at the perfect landscaping and the subtle exterior lighting showing off the architecture, the front door opened and a stunning woman strolled out. A gorgeous blue dress clung to her voluptuous body and a pleased smile curved her full lips.

'Who's that?' She gasped involuntarily.

She heard the muttered oath beneath Theo's breath and he swiftly got out of the car. The rhythm of the stunning woman's high-heeled shoes bumped unevenly when she saw Leah emerge and stand just behind Theo.

'Angelica.' Theo bestowed kisses on the woman's cheeks. 'I'm sorry I wasn't here to greet you properly—'

The woman purred something in Greek.

'Leah.' Theo turned, still speaking in English to include her. 'May I introduce you to our good family friend, Angelica Galanis?'

Family friend? Was that what she was?

'Angelica, this is Leah.'

But Theo didn't give Angelica any additional explanation of Leah.

A low cough made all three of them turn. An elderly man with a cane was in the open doorway. Leah froze. This just had to be Dimitri. While he was shorter than Theo and frail, he had a familiar steely look in his gaze. Leah surreptitiously wiped her hands on her jeans. She felt crumpled and stale and never more out of place. And she'd been out of place a lot.

'Theodoros?' The older man looked from Theo to Leah.

'Dimitri.' Theo clamped Leah's hand in his and walked towards the waiting man. 'I wanted to introduce you formally tomorrow, but this is wonderful. I am pleased to introduce you to Leah.'

Dimitri simply stared.

'Leah is my fiancée.'

She heard the muffled gasp of surprise from the woman just behind them. Dimitri said nothing to her directly but whispered a short comment to Theo. Theo wrapped his arm around Leah's waist and pulled her close. The old man's breathing became ragged and Theo spoke to him in reassuring tones before lifting his voice to call something in Greek.

An older woman immediately appeared behind Dimitri. Given her deferential manner, Leah guessed she was on the staff. Theo quietly spoke to the woman and a moment later she escorted Dimitri down a long corridor lined with large portraits. Even through the thick walls Leah could sense the older man's emotion—it was strong enough to reverberate all the way through her own ribcage.

'My grandfather is still recovering from his operation,' Theo said smoothly and guided her into the polished foyer. He smiled at her as if there were nothing at all awkward about the situation—as if they were truly intimate. 'We'll spend time with him properly tomorrow.'

'Theo, it's very late and obviously not the right time for you to have a house guest.' Angelica's face was flushed and her English was heavily accented. 'I should probably go...' She trailed off.

'It's late, please stay tonight and we'll make travel arrangements for you in the morning,' Theo replied smoothly.

Despite his charming exterior, Leah could sense his underlying tension too. The 'welcome home' committee seemed to have exacerbated it.

'I apologise again for not being here to welcome you properly,' he said to Angelica. 'But thank you for understanding this is a personal time for us.'

Theo stiffened as Angelica's gaze lingered on the glittering ring on Leah's finger. He stepped between the two women, protecting Leah from Angelica's scrutiny. She was paler than usual and she'd half turned away; defensiveness seeped from her hunched shoulders. It was as if she was trying to be that shadow as he'd suggested on the plane. She'd been hurt before. Having met her parents, he understood more. But she ought to stand tall. He didn't want her to feel any fear, any inferiority here. 'Are you hungry, Leah?' he asked gently.

She shook her head.

He held out his hand to her. 'Come, I'll take you to our quarters.'

She put her hand in his and he turned and bowed to Angelica. He'd clean forgotten the woman was coming to visit and of course Dimitri would have stayed up to welcome him with his guest. Instead now Dimitri was tired and shocked. Theo couldn't blame him. Tomorrow he'd ensure the old man believed he and Leah were happy. While he hated lying, he didn't want Dimitri to know he'd messed up.

And now there was Leah. He knew he had to give her some space and a chance to take all this in. She hadn't wanted to stay in touch after that night at the hotel. She hadn't even wanted to kiss him goodbye. Now he'd dragged her to a foreign country where she didn't speak the language and she'd been given an awkward welcome. He'd almost done to her what had been done to him all those years ago and he was furious with himself.

That large diamond dug into his palm as he clasped her fingers and led her to the stairs. He felt a heel about the blunt way he'd just handed that to her too. But he refused to lie to her. It was imperative he maintain distance between them. He'd start as he meant to go on.

Except all he wanted to do was kiss away the sad tilt to her mouth and restore that passionate warmth in her eyes. He wanted to hear her husky little laugh again.

'This is my suite.' He opened the door to his private wing and waited for her to walk in.

'Angelica is an old family friend?' There was no missing the suspicious curiosity in her eyes.

'I forgot Dimitri had invited her to stay this weekend. If I'd remembered I would have cancelled the invitation.' He gritted his teeth.

'Is it a special occasion?'

'Not that I'm aware of.'

'Why had he invited her?'

He closed the door behind them. 'Why do you think?'

'Your grandfather invited her to stay with you as a prospective what—bride?' She frowned. 'He doesn't trust you to pick a woman on your own?'

'He doesn't trust that I'll ever make a *permanent* pick,' Theo said tightly. 'I was keeping him happy while he recovers.'

'Keeping him happy?' she echoed. 'Because you never wanted to get married.'

'Actually now I do. To you.' He made himself walk forward and open the door to her bedroom.

She came to an abrupt halt and spun to face him. 'You expect me to sleep in the same bed as you?'

He glanced and saw the big bed behind her. Her tone pushed him that last notch over the edge. Now he was alone with her again at last desire washed over him, loosening the bonds of self-control he'd been straining against for hours. In truth, for months. He'd wanted her the second he'd seen her again. He'd never stopped wanting her since that night. The whole 'I'm pregnant' thing ought to have shut it down. It hadn't.

'Is this for the look of it, Theo?' She jerked her head towards the bed. 'Because there are other people here?'

He couldn't control himself enough to reply. It was a mistake, because in the face of his silence, he felt her emotions fire.

'I can play that part if you want.' She flicked back her hair and stepped up to him, her lavender eyes deepening with almost liquid intensity. 'I'll jump up and down on that bed and scream with ecstasy all through the house so everyone in the neighbourhood hears. I'll—'

'Be amazing?' he challenged, his body almost bursting with the feral energy he'd held leashed for so long. 'Bring it on.'

She jerked her chin at him defiantly. 'You think you can just order me around? That I'll do *anything* you ask me to?'

He breathed hard but those knots were slipping. He *did* want her to do anything and her loss of temper was oddly welcome. It had been a long, trying day and both of them needed to vent. But he was *not* the villain here.

'My grandfather's rooms are in another building on the other side of the tennis court. Angelica is in the guest house on the other side of the pool. You can be as loud as you like.'

He'd jump her on the bed with him if she wanted. And he'd happily make her scream.

'If they're that far away, then why do I need to be in your room?'

'You don't,' he snapped. 'This is my *wing*, Leah. There's more than one bedroom in here.'

She gaped and then a flush swept up her face. 'Why? For your secret harem?'

He laughed roughly at her temper and inwardly revelled at the way the colour made her radiance return. She looked so much more alive than the cautious woman of only moments earlier.

'Stop being so poisonous.' He stepped closer, unable to keep any distance at all. 'We slept in separate rooms last night, remember? I'm not about to insist that change. Or is it that you want to be back in my bed?'

Was that what it was? Now they had privacy, she could voice her thoughts. And now that she was beyond provoked, she'd revealed what was uppermost in her mind.

'What? *No!*' But her mouth formed a full-lipped pout and her purple-tinged eyes shimmered with passion.

Sizzling sexual tension pulled him closer still. They'd have separate lives, yes, but maybe clearing this heated fog might be the best thing for them both. He didn't want to fight. Didn't want anything else from her... But *this*? The pull was undeniable.

'You want to be back there every bit as much as I want you there,' he muttered.

'If you think I want you—'

'You're not a good liar, sweetheart. You've told me that yourself.' He couldn't resist a second longer. Reaching out, he cupped her jaw.

'Theo...'

Satisfaction merged with desire at her soft whisper of submission and the gentle lean into his touch. His need had such power, he was driven to kiss, not her mouth, but that delicate, sensitive skin of her neck. He'd take more, touch more, do everything unexpected and delightful. She shivered, her hands lifted, not to push him away but to clutch his shirt and pull him closer still. This was what he wanted. Her embrace, her smile, her playfulness.

Her soft moan made him giddy with triumph and the diabolical desire to tease her overpowered him.

'Oh, no,' he said as he nibbled his way down. He wanted her as tortured as he'd been these last weeks and then he wanted to assuage it. 'No screaming your ecstasy,' he softly echoed her taunt. 'You've got to be quiet. If you're not quiet, I'm going to stop.'

'You're not going to start,' she muttered breathlessly.

'I already have and you're already ahead of me.'

'You arrogant…'

But she trailed off as his fingers traced the neckline of her loose tee.

'I might be arrogant but I'm not wrong.' He pulled her fully into his embrace. 'Be quiet, Leah. Or I stop.'

Leah knew she could say no and he'd stop. She could say anything and he'd stop. But the last thing she wanted was for him to stop. So, instead, she smiled.

He kissed along her cheekbones, then her eyelids so she closed her eyes. His fingertips teased and she moaned again. Her skin was so sensitive to his touch. She heard his muttered oath, a mumble of something hot and ferocious, and then his hands lifted her. He swiftly crossed the floor to the bed and tumbled down onto it with her. She cried out with the powerful pleasure of being with him like this again. Of having him above her, caressing her, pinning her with his magnificent body.

'You don't want me to stop, do you?' he whispered hotly against her mouth.

She kept silent but arched her hips to meet his—uncaring about the layers of clothes between them. She just needed to feel him. She sought him the one way she could—with her body, closing her mind to any more repercussions. His laugh was smothered on her skin as he kissed down her torso, lifting her tee out of his way with his teeth. But he wouldn't let her touch him back. He kept her too busy squirming, seeking more of his wicked mouth. She shook with need. He traced his hand carefully over her, making her quiver. She gasped as his hand easily slipped beneath the loose waistband of her jeans, then deeper to where she was slick and hot. She heard his harshly drawn breath as he discovered just how much she wanted him. She didn't care how much she was feeding his ego with her response right now. She didn't care that he now knew he could do whatever he wanted, whenever he wanted, if he wanted. She was too needy.

'Theo—' She shivered, desperately biting her lip. She didn't want him to stop but she couldn't hold back her cry.

He looked into her eyes. His were filled with tender heat as he stroked her with a firm but gentle touch. 'Let it out, sweetheart,' he muttered roughly. 'I want to hear you, want to see you, want to feel you.' His groan was soul-filled. 'I have missed you.'

Any game was forgotten, burned to cinders by the honesty in that scorching whisper. An outpouring of warmth and want flooded her. He didn't give her a chance to answer, or himself an opportunity to say anything more, because he kissed her—so thoroughly, so passionately, while his fingers teased her to the point of no return. She arched—high and taut, straining for the release only he could bring.

'Leah.' He broke free and breathed.

'Yes!' She convulsed, her cry echoing as her whole world was obliterated.

She drowned in the tumultuous sensations, utterly, utterly undone. She couldn't find the energy to open her eyes and she didn't want to. She wanted to stay in this half-dream-state of delight.

I have missed you.

That whispered secret had felled her. She'd missed him too. She'd missed this closeness. This easiness. But now total exhaustion scrubbed her ability to do anything—to speak, move, think. She wanted to open her eyes but she couldn't. She felt him brush her hair from her face, then he gently repeated the motion again, then again. Until Leah discovered she couldn't resist anything any more—not him. Nor the pull of a profound sleep.

CHAPTER EIGHT

LEAH FURIOUSLY SCRUBBED her body, rejecting the lingering warmth from last night and trying not to appreciate the stunning luxury of the gleaming marble bathroom. Despite that wide blue sky and brilliant sunshine outside, her mood was bad because when she'd woken she'd discovered he wasn't there. It wasn't the fact that he wasn't there that made her disgruntled. It was that she'd *wanted* him to be there. If he'd really missed her, why had he left so early? Or was it just that he'd missed *sex*?

Had he only touched her because she'd provoked him? Because he was venting the frustrations of a very long day? Except he'd not asked for anything for himself after her release. He'd merely proved his power over her and then he'd stayed and stroked her hair and that was mortifying. She had no idea when he'd left her, only that he had. She'd woken, still half dressed, not even in the bed but on top of it and covered by a light blanket that he must have put over her.

She swiftly towelled dry, pulled on a fresh tee and jeans and then glanced out of the window at that incredible view again. There was a gorgeous lap pool with guest houses on both sides and, beyond that, the crystalline sea stretched for miles. It was the bluest water she'd ever seen.

But now she could see Theo and Angelica seated at a big table on the terrace. Theo was in trousers and white shirt, his sleeves rolled back enough to show off his tanned forearms. She clamped down on that restless ache.

Angelica wore another stunning summery dress, her hair and make-up immaculate. She was clearly at ease with having staff serve breakfast, felt no awkwardness in wondering what to say or how to say it. The fact was, they looked good together. Leah was nothing like that woman. She wasn't Greek. Or beautiful. Or from the 'right society'. She was a pregnant nobody, with no qualifications, no real achievements to date. Her black jeans and black tee were too old, loose and casual—they didn't fit the scene. And nor did the rest of her. She froze, not wanting to go down and join them. She didn't think she could fake it.

Pull it together.

She had to get over herself. He'd taken her by the hand, he'd introduced her as his fiancée. If she chose not to go down there now, then wasn't *she* choosing to be invisible again? For so long she'd wanted to escape that doormat role; she couldn't revert to it just because she was scared. She had to do better for her baby and make this work.

By the time Leah made it down to the ground floor Angelica was standing ready for departure. 'It was fascinating to meet you, Leah,' she said. 'I'm sure we'll see each other again.'

Despite that polite farewell, there was no mistaking Angelica's sharp curiosity. Leah fought the instinct to cover her belly. She turned towards the terrace as Theo guided Angelica to the car. She'd fuel up, ready to face his family.

Theo watched the car head down the drive, taking Angelica away. No doubt she'd tell everyone about the woman he'd brought back with him. His instinctive need to protect Leah built, but he'd face Dimitri first. Their meetings usually didn't go much beyond balance sheets and brainstorming business expansions. They lived and breathed the banking business and their unspoken agreement had cemented over the years—

they never discussed the past. But while Theo had protected the old man for so long, he couldn't have him hate Leah.

'Tell me about her,' Dimitri said quietly when Theo went to the old man's study to explain.

Theo thought about the way she supported her ballet friend, her brother, those elderly residents at that home. 'She's very caring.' But he braced—there was no point prevaricating. 'She's pregnant.'

Dimitri didn't move.

'You'll make her welcome,' he added, wondering if that man had even heard what he'd said. 'I am responsible for her.'

To his total astonishment and total discomfort, Dimitri's eyes filled.

'She's having your child?' the old man clarified.

'Yes.' He still had to steel himself to admit it aloud, let alone prepare for the reaction he was about to get.

'I didn't think…' The old man breathed out. 'Good, Theo.'

Good? Theo blinked, gobsmacked by the old man's obvious emotion. *Good?*

'She will have my great-grandson.' Pride lit the old man's face.

Theo still couldn't stand to imagine an actual baby, but at Dimitri's satisfied certainty he couldn't help a small tease. 'Or great-granddaughter.'

'Wonderful.' Dimitri actually beamed at the prospect. 'Then you'd better go take care of her.'

No more questions? No desire to know more? No judgment? Theo couldn't believe it.

Hurting more somehow, he pushed away the previously unimaginable mental picture of Dimitri hovering over a bundle in Leah's arms. He felt as if he were skating on the thinnest of ice. With one wrong move, it would crack and they'd be dragged down to drown in frigid waters. But if he kept his steps careful, they could all stay safe.

She was standing by the pool. How could such a slender silhouette be such a distraction? Such temptation. His pulse quickened at the memory of late last night. But as he registered her pale façade, regret rose. She'd been tired last night and she'd misunderstood about the bedroom and he shouldn't have taken advantage of her innocence and anger and emotional vulnerability to satisfy his own needs. He'd lost control, no longer able to resist the desire to touch her. All he'd wanted was to lose himself with her again. He'd only hauled his control back when she'd all but fainted away in an exhausted heap after her orgasm had hit. A fact that had made him feel all the more guilty.

They had to focus on getting their marriage arranged and to provide security for the child. The paperwork for the wedding was in hand so it was simply a matter of getting through the next few days. Once they were married, they could take a breath and figure out the future more gently. Until then, *he* needed to regain control.

'How did you sleep?' he asked, even though it was obvious in her expression.

'Very well, thank you.' She lifted her chin. 'I realise now that you were just helping me to... relax.' She breathed in. 'Thank you for that. It was thoughtful.' She glanced at the table. 'But I'll manage with just a glass of warm milk from now on.'

A glass of milk? He stared. She couldn't be serious. And as for him helping her to relax? As if there'd been any thought that had gone before what had happened?

Her coolness sparked his desire to prove her a liar all over again. His desire simply to touch her again. He was appalled at the realisation he had zero control. *Zero.* All he wanted was to get close again and know that starburst of heat. But he rejected the want winding him tight. He'd go to the office in Athens. Bury himself in the work he'd missed while he was London collecting her. He'd regain focus and get ahead. When in doubt, achieve.

At that thought, a great wave of resistance rose. How much he wanted to stay scared him. He never wanted to skip work. It was always his escape. But now?

'I need to go into the office,' he said brusquely before he could change his mind.

'Today?'

'I had an extra day in the UK. I need to catch up.' He was good at doing what was necessary and *this* was necessary.

'Because you're so behind from one extra day away?' Her lashes hid the glittering sharpness of her eyes.

'I'll be back in time for dinner.' He needed distance. She was already paying too steep a price for his reckless behaviour and he couldn't trust himself not to repeat it.

'And what do you want me to do while you're gone?' she asked softly.

'Rest, Leah. You need it.' He'd go to work. After their wedding he'd take her to the island

and show her that life wasn't going to be a total disaster.

'I need it?'

There was only a lone ember of provocation in her soft echo, but he couldn't resist throwing one last little retaliation as he forced his feet to take him away. 'Go have that hot milk and relax.'

Leah stomped back into the mansion. How was she supposed to 'relax'? What was she supposed to do with her time? She knew no one but Theo and she didn't know him at all well. His grandfather hadn't appeared since last night. She wasn't sure he even spoke much English and she certainly couldn't speak Greek. She had no transport options, no map of the city anyway and no money. Sure, she could swim in that pool, but she had no swimsuit and she wasn't sure skinny dipping would be a good idea. Worse, she realised Theo might've been right: her jeans collection wasn't going to cut it. She needed clothing appropriate enough to mix with the Angelicas of Athens. Not dresses though. Leah didn't wear dresses...

She could eat from the platters of nibbles that constantly appeared on the nearest occasional table but she was too wound up to have any appetite. She could sleep up in that gorgeous bedroom but she only needed to set foot in there and all the memories of his touch tormented her. She could definitely read because she'd discovered there were books everywhere, not just in the stunning library. There was a home movie theatre too and a ballroom that was beautiful but wistfully empty. It was a grand home for a large family and she ought to feel amazing. Instead she literally walked away from it all. But as she reached a path that she guessed led to the beach, a security guy materialised in front of her. She stopped and smiled at him warily.

'If you would like to walk along the beach, I will escort you,' he said briskly in heavily accented English.

'Oh, no, thank you.' She backed up a pace. 'Sorry if I bothered you.'

There was no return smile. 'I'm here to ensure your safety.'

'Oh, okay. Thank you.'

So there were boundaries to this world? She marched back inside feeling odd about not being able to come and go alone as she pleased. She'd get her knitting. It seemed ridiculous to be working with wool in such warm weather but it always relaxed her. And she really needed to relax.

She walked along the corridor and glanced again at the collection of formal portraits that hung so prominently positioned. There was a wedding portrait of Dimitri and his wife, and another of that woman alone, looking a little older. Then there was a portrait of a younger man Leah suspected was Theo's father. He looked no older than about fifteen. There was no portrait from his wedding, indeed there was no image at all of Theo's mother. And then there was the one of Theo and Dimitri together. Theo looked about eighteen. Both he and Dimitri were in suits, formally posed. There was no smile and man-hug. They stood separate, angled in front of a large desk. It looked as if it had been taken at an office. Theo's first day at work? Had he been groomed to be the head of the Savas empire from the start? What about his father? Because there was no equivalent 'line of succession' photo of him. Her curiosity deepened. Theo hadn't mentioned his mother at all in his brief explanation of why he'd come to live with Dimitri. And it had been a *very* brief explanation.

She gathered her bag from her room and returned poolside to lose herself in the blissfully soothing repetition of stitch after stitch. She wasn't interrupted—other than with trays of food—but slowly, inexorably, her nerves tightened. When would he return home? They had to talk some more, surely. She couldn't spend all her days like this.

He phoned her late in the afternoon.

'I won't be back until after dinner tonight,' he said brusquely as soon as she answered. 'Don't wait up.'

The businesslike way he delivered the minimal message was chilling. And that disappointment? She didn't want to admit to that at all.

The early evening stretched out—slow and painful. She saw Dimitri in the distance but he didn't come near her and frankly now she was too intimidated and heartsore to face someone else's disappointment or judgment. She asked the housekeeper if she could dine alone in her bedroom. Of course it was no problem.

In safe, private misery she flicked on the television in the small lounge simply because she had nothing better to do. She scrolled through the channels, pausing on what she guessed was the local news channel. They were showing a live feed from the waterfront just up the coast. Intrigued, she watched for a while; it looked like the cream of Athens society—all the gorgeous Angelicas. But then she stared harder at the screen. Was that *Theo*?

She blinked. It *was*. She'd recognise his height and imposing presence from fifty feet and he was dressed to disturb in dinner jacket and white tie. And there were women near him—beautiful, designer-clad beauties. Was this what he considered *work*? Quaffing champagne down at some fancy marina?

She stilled, unsure what to do, quelling the urge to phone him. She waited for his return but in the end fell asleep before she heard his car. In the morning she expected to see him at breakfast, but there was still no sign. It was the housekeeper who informed her with a slightly confused air that he was already at work. That was when Leah realised he'd not returned home all night. Hurt burgeoned—built by his lack of consideration, of contact. Was this what it was going to be like? How could he go from concerned and courteous to simply…absent?

She wanted him to see her as she'd thought he once had. She didn't want to be invisible and taken for granted again.

As the day passed in isolation, her hurt festered, morphing into fury. By the time he finally returned, *after* dinner, she was practically shaking with pent-up rage. She'd hidden away in her room again, not wanting anyone to witness their 'reunion'.

She heard his footsteps as he climbed the stairs—she'd left her door ajar so she'd be forewarned. Now he nudged her door further open with his fingers.

'Nice of you to call in,' she said acidly, loathing her shrewish tone but unable to hold it back.

'I told you I had to work late yesterday.' He leaned against the doorjamb and regarded her carefully. 'It got so late it was best for me to stay in town.'

'You really think I'm stupid, don't you?' She was so hurt.

'Why do you say that?'

'You weren't at "work" last night. You were at a party.' He was avoiding her. He'd been avoiding her for the last couple of days.

'Actually, it wasn't a party. It was the launch of a new yacht.'

'Is this what it's going to be like? You're just going to lie by omission...or semantics? Like how you treat your grandfather? You let him think the best through half-truths, to kid yourself you're keeping him happy? Is that what you're planning to do with me?'

He straightened and came into the room, closing the door behind him. 'I'm not lying at all to you.' He gazed at her steadily and walked slowly towards her. 'I've never lied to you.'

'No, you're just planning to send me away so you can pretend I don't exist most of the time.' She sprang up and stepped away, putting the armchair safely between him and her. 'That's why you're not involving me in any of your life here. Lock me in the attic, why don't you?'

'Leah—'

'Don't patronise me or act like you're trying to protect me. Why not just tell me the truth?' She shook her head.

'It was work. I'm the CEO of one of the largest private banks in the world and we have several subsidiaries in a variety of industries. Patronage, sponsorship, networking are all part of the remit. We're powerful, we need to contribute to society. So it's part of my job to maintain the profile and reputation at a certain level. To develop the goodwill and trust of investors and clients.'

'Is that why you didn't want me there? Because I'm not going to maintain the reputation of you or your family or your precious business?'

'Would you really want to go?' He looked surprised. 'You're in no state to be out there yet—you're exhausted. You don't speak the language or—'

'Look the part?'

'Or have the knowledge to deal with these people. *Yet.*' He put his hands on his hips and gazed at her. 'Give us some time, Leah.'

The injustice of that comment made her flare. 'You're the one not giving us any *time*, Theo. You're using work to avoid me. And your grandfather. I might not be able to negotiate billion-dollar deals but attending a *party* hardly requires a master's in rocket science. It's not hard to talk to people.' She glared at him. 'Yet it seems that, for you, talking is really hard. Why didn't you ask me?'

'Perhaps I should have.'

'Perhaps? You just want to hide me away on your prison island.'

'It's *not* a prison.' He actually laughed.

'You don't want me to be seen.' She tossed her head, refusing to let his humour placate her. 'But I'm used to people looking at me and judging. I can ignore them.'

A frown formed on his face. 'What do you think they see?'

She didn't want to think about this. 'I can't care

about what they see or think. I won't be hidden away like something to be ashamed of. Not by the man I'm going to marry.'

She couldn't be treated as if she were inferior or an embarrassment. She'd had enough of that in her life already.

'Is that what you thought I was doing?' He took in a deep breath. 'Leah, while we're married, I'll never humiliate you. I'll never cheat on you. I will be loyal.'

But she wanted more than integrity. She wanted so much more that she dared not think about. 'How many properties do you have?' she asked desperately.

'Does it matter?'

'Where are they? Perhaps there's a destination that might suit me better. Paris? New York? I'd quite like to live in Manhattan.'

'You'll be within a thirty-minute flight distance from me,' he said grimly.

'Thirty minutes?'

'I just want to protect you,' he said. 'And the child,' he added belatedly.

'From what? What's so awful about Athens that we have to be locked away on Prison Island?'

He folded his arms. 'I just want you to have the privacy and space to be happy.'

'You mean *you* want privacy and space away from us most of the time. You'll just swoop in on the weekends and be the fun guy and then leave.'

'The fun guy?' He looked stunned for a second, then sobered again. 'That's not what it's about. Dimitri needs to believe that we're happy. For as long as he's alive, you and I are happy.'

'He's not stupid. If we're living apart most of the time, he'll suspect we're not happy.'

'But if we're together all the time he'll be *certain* we're unhappy. Always having to show a happy façade is impossible.'

A happy *façade*? Was it beyond the realms of possibility that they could actually *be* happy? Couldn't this feeling become something else? Something more? Or was she really totally alone in thinking there *was* this feeling? There was something linking them together.

'I'll visit you on the weekends but we'd have space and privacy there and wouldn't have to carry on an act in front of him. You can rest.'

'Do I want to rest?' She exploded. Had he been carrying on an act when he'd touched her so intimately last night? When he'd told her he missed her? 'Maybe I want to live life.'

'And you will.' He paced away from her. 'I'm not trying to hide you away.'

'No? Then why have you brought me here and left me alone?'

'I...' He flexed his hands. 'I'm trying to get my head around everything.'

'And I'm not? Can't we do this *together*, Theo?' She tried to break through his barriers. 'I don't want someone making all the decisions as if I have nothing of value to contribute.'

'That wasn't my intention.' He shifted and pivoted to face her again. 'You want more from me.'

'Some communication,' she muttered. 'Some discussion.'

'All right.' He sighed and reached out as if he could no longer resist, gently rubbing his fingertip along her jaw. 'Leah...'

She turned helplessly into his touch, hating herself as she did. 'Don't use my weakness to distract me.'

His eyebrows lifted. '*Your* weakness?'

She closed her eyes. 'This wasn't what I meant when I said I wanted more from you.'

He drew an audible breath. 'Do you think it's only you who wants...this?' He sounded almost choked. 'But I can't be the kind of husband you should have.'

She opened her eyes and gazed straight into his. 'Why would you think that?'

He froze, a rigid expression masked his thoughts. Again she realised he was battling something deep inside—something painful.

'You're kind, Theo. I know you'll support me. You've said you'll be faithful and I believe you. What else do you think a husband needs to do?'

He was so rigid she grew wary of his answer.

'I can't love you, Leah.'

She stilled, shocked by his quiet, so calm confession.

'I can't love anyone,' he added huskily.

His eyes flashed with sorry sincerity and seemed to ask for her forgiveness. But why would he say that?

'You love your grandfather,' she whispered. She'd seen it. Almost everything he did, he did with that man in mind.

'I *owe* my grandfather,' he corrected softly and stepped back. 'I'm sorry, Leah.'

CHAPTER NINE

RETURNING FROM A lonely breakfast the next day, Leah paused on the threshold of her room. The housekeeper was in there, carefully folding Leah's cardigan.

'Thank you,' Leah said shyly, aware there wasn't a lot of warmth in the woman's face. 'We haven't properly met—my name is Leah.'

She hadn't been introduced to anyone properly yet. Theo had been in too much of a rush to deal with his work crisis and it seemed none of his staff were overly friendly.

'Amalia.'

Leah offered her a smile and saw the way she was looking at the ribbed pattern on her cardigan. 'Do you knit?'

Amalia glanced, her expression softening. 'I make lace.'

'Oh.' Leah stepped closer, her interest flaring. 'I'd love to watch you some time…' She trailed off awkwardly. Perhaps it wasn't the done thing to chat?

But then Amalia smiled and gestured at the cardigan. 'Did you make this?'

'I did, yes.' Leah smiled. 'I knit a lot—it relaxes me. Though I probably won't need to as much. It's very warm here...'

She trailed off again. She was babbling—nervous and awkward and too eager to engage in desperately needed social contact.

But Amalia finally smiled. 'It can get cold here in winter.'

'Does it?'

'It even snows in Athens—'

'No.' She'd had no idea.

Amalia laughed and nodded.

Encouraged, Leah nibbled her lip but then smiled. 'Actually, I need to buy some clothes,' she said. She needed to look the part as best she could. She needed to make an effort to embrace the country and culture her child was going to be born into. 'Would you be able to help me? Come with me?'

'Shopping?' Amalia looked startled.

'Yes.' Leah nodded hopefully. 'I have no idea where to go.' Or what to get.

Amalia looked pleased. 'Of course—'

'Oh, thank you,' she breathed out with a rush of relief. 'And I need a wedding dress...'

'You wouldn't make one?' Amalia gestured at Leah's bag. 'You could knit with silk.'

Leah's smile blossomed. 'I've love to.' She'd been working on a pattern for a while—a dress of her own design she *would* wear. 'But I don't have enough time before the wedding.'

'What if I helped you? I have lace...'

'You'd do that?' Leah was stunned.

Amalia straightened. 'You're marrying Theodoros.'

Of course, this was about Theo. Did Amalia care for him? Theo worked so hard, he was a dutiful grandson and a good boss...maybe Amalia and the other staff weren't only wary while they decided whether she was good enough for him? Were they protective of him? Why? Because they loved him? She had the feeling he was very easy to love.

'You know him well?' she asked gently, hoping she was hiding how curious she was about him. Why did he have this huge sense of duty but total denial of love? Why did he think he was incapable of it? She didn't believe him. She couldn't when his actions said so much otherwise. She was sure he always tried to do what was best for those he was close to. He'd do that for their baby too, wouldn't he? She *had* to believe that.

'I've worked for Dimitri for years,' Amalia said. 'My husband too.'

'Really?'

Amalia smiled. 'And my sons did too, before they went away to study.'

'So you were here when Theo arrived?' Leah asked cautiously.

'Yes.' Amalia glanced at her, as if she knew there were a million more questions on Leah's tongue. 'He was very quiet when he first arrived.'

Leah held her breath, not wanting to interrupt Amalia and stop her, wondering why Theo had been so quiet. Had he been afraid?

'He had little Greek, of course,' Amalia said. 'But he studied very hard. He has always worked very hard.'

Always? Hadn't he got up to mischief like most teenagers? Hadn't he ever rebelled?

I owe my grandfather.

Perhaps not. Had he always been so determined to pay him back? Why? Wasn't it natural for a grandfather to take in a grandson when his parents had gone? But where had his mother gone?

'I'll arrange the driver if you would like to go shopping now,' Amalia said, interrupting Leah's thoughts. 'Ten minutes, okay?'

'Perfect. *Thank you.*'

The plan put a lift in Leah's step, but when she came downstairs a few minutes later to find Amalia, Dimitri was sitting in the living room.

'Amalia is taking you shopping,' he said without preamble.

'Yes.' She automatically moved to adjust the cushion that was awkwardly positioned behind him.

'You want to spend money?' he asked warily when she'd fixed it and stepped back.

'Yes.' She smiled, battling hard not to be afraid of him. It was their first proper conversation and he was openly questioning her motives.

But she didn't blame him for not trusting her yet.

'I need something suitable when I meet Theo's business colleagues. I don't want to let him down.' And that was the truth. She wanted to please both Theo and his grandfather.

But Dimitri's demeanour didn't thaw.

Leah worried her lip and made herself ask the honest question. 'Do you think I'm after his money?'

'Aren't you?'

She paused. So much for Theo convincing him that their engagement was a love match.

'No,' she said firmly. 'I'm here because he insisted on it.' She swallowed and sat in the chair opposite his. 'I don't know Athens at all, in fact this is my first time to Greece. And I'm sorry if my arrival is a surprise to you. But I think we both want the best for Theo. I'm having his baby and I most definitely want the best for my child. But to be honest, I need some help.'

His expression finally softened.

'I don't speak any Greek,' she confessed in a relieved rush. 'Do you think Amalia can help me find a tutor?'

'You want to learn Greek?'

'Of course.' She was going to be living here for the foreseeable future, she didn't want to feel isolated from everyone for ever and she wanted her baby to enjoy its dual heritage. 'It might take me a while though,' she admitted with a sudden laugh. 'I'm not very academic.'

'I will help you.' He nodded slowly.

'You will?' She beamed at him. 'Thank you.'

He shot her a look. 'Thank you. *Efharisto*.' He then waited, looking at her expectantly.

'You mean *you'll* help me?' she asked. Dimitri himself?

'Thank you. *Efharisto,*' he repeated.

'Efharisto?'

'Yes. *Ne.*' He suddenly clapped his hands and called to Amalia. 'Come, you will speak to her only in Greek. Greek all the time.'

'Ne, Dimitri.' Amalia smiled and gestured for Leah to follow her.

Fortunately, Amalia disregarded Dimitri's order while they shopped. But *unfortunately* Amalia simply smiled and said yes to everything Leah tried on in the high-end boutiques of Athens. It was sweet and supportive, but truly not that helpful.

Theo had said she'd hidden behind her black clothing and perhaps he was right. She'd tried to avoid that backlash because of her height and slenderness. But maybe she should enjoy all the colours she loved and had always turned away from? Not just scarlet panties…

Not for him. For herself, right?

Except really, she realised it was *because* of him. He'd *seen* her that night and he'd liked what he'd seen. And she'd liked the person he'd made her feel free to be. The person confident enough to speak up for what she wanted with him. Confident to speak up to her parents for once. The person confident to call *him* to account too... She glanced again at the racks of clothing and turned her back on the black.

Three hours into the reinvigorated shopping marathon, her phone rang.

'Will you accompany me to an exhibition tonight?' Theo said.

'Pardon?'

'A driver will collect you at seven.' He paused. 'If you would like, that is.' She heard his smile. 'I am trying to ask, not dictate.'

'Okay,' she agreed cautiously, yet her heart raced because he'd listened and he was trying to include her. A fragile bubble bloomed—if he could try like this, maybe he could open up even more? Maybe he might even develop deeper feelings? She shivered, pushing away that wisp of a wish—*one day at a time.*

'I'm busy with meetings until late and I'll get changed at the office,' he said.

She glanced at the silky fabric hanging in front of her. 'I don't wear dresses, Theo.'

'Nor do I.' He laughed. 'Will you be ready?'

'Yes.'

Hours later she avidly stared out of the window, drinking in the sights as she was driven into the centre of Athens. Theo was waiting outside the gallery. Bowled over by the sight of him in that black tuxedo, she braced, slamming back her nerves. She was *not* concerned by his silent scrutiny.

'We need to—' He broke off and cleared his throat.

'To?'

'Walk inside.'

'I believe I'm capable of that,' she said with a shy laugh. 'Are you?'

He cleared his throat again. 'Scarlet, Leah?'

'Is it okay?'

'Does it need to be?' He finally smiled. 'You don't need my approval.'

'Maybe I would like it.'

He took her hand and drew her close to his side. 'It's not my approval you have, Leah. It's something else. Something raw. Something I can't deny. Something I can't turn off.' He breathed out. 'Who did your make-up?'

'I did.'

'You have skills.'

'I didn't let my mother stop me doing everything I was interested in. I just did it in secret. Sometimes.'

'What else did you do in secret?'

She just smiled at him and shrugged.

'I'm glad you're not doing it in secret now,' he admitted. 'I'm glad you're here letting the world see you.'

'They're seeing all right,' she noted with a wry grimace and her nerves mushroomed. 'They're staring.'

He cocked his head and blinked at her with teasing arrogance. 'What makes you think they're staring at you? I'm the one they're interested in.'

She choked on a giggle. 'Good point.'

'No.' He shook his head. 'They're staring because you look stunning.'

Heat travelled all over her body and he wrapped his arm around her to draw her closer.

'What are you doing?' she half gasped.

'You're the one who wanted to be treated like my fiancée.' He brushed a kiss against her cheek. 'This is how I'd do that. I'd stay close and kiss her often.'

'No, you wouldn't,' she breathed. 'That's not dignified enough for your grandfather.'

'You think I'm too uptight for displays of affection?'

'I think you're conscious of your position and

you modify your behaviour depending on who's around.'

'Doesn't everyone?' He laughed. 'Isn't that just good manners?'

'But people still do what they want. They put themselves first. I don't know that you do.'

'Haven't I done that with you once already?' He stilled and faced her. 'You want me to put my desires first and damn who's watching? Damn the consequences?'

'Can you?'

He cupped the nape of her neck, pulled her to him and kissed her. It was a long, luscious kiss.

He lifted his head and laughed down at her dazed expression. 'You dared me to.'

She shook her head. 'That was just part of your PR plan. You weren't taking me seriously.'

'If I did what I really wanted right now, we'd both be arrested.'

She felt his hard heat digging into her pelvis.

'So now we have a problem,' he muttered hotly. 'I need you right here to preserve my blushes in front of all these people, but if you stay there, my little problem isn't going to go away.'

'*Little* problem?' she echoed archly.

'It's a good thing you're wearing trousers. If it was a skirt I'd have flipped it up and bent you over that piano already.' He grinned at her gasp. 'Sorry. Too honest?' His smile faded. 'I want you too much.'

'You've got some of my lipstick.' She gestured to her mouth, mirroring the placement of the smudge.

'So help me.' His slightly strangled-sounding request was oddly serious.

'Theo Savas.' A man interrupted them loudly and Theo instantly straightened, his expression smoothing back to reserved.

'You can't return to Athens and hide in the corner all evening.' The stranger's gaze skimmed over Leah, his eyes widening. 'And you are?'

'Leah Turner, my fiancée,' Theo answered for her.

'So the crazy rumours are correct?' The man stared back at Theo.

'They're not crazy,' Theo said coldly.

Rather rudely the man switched to Greek but frankly Leah was glad she didn't have to listen. She extracted herself from Theo's hold and with a small smile at him stepped aside to view the nearest painting.

As soon as she did, a designer-clad, stunningly polished woman swept over to her. 'You're Leah, aren't you? Theo Savas' fiancée.'

'That's correct.' She smiled. 'And you are?'

'Phoebe, a friend of Theo's. We're delighted and intrigued that you could join us. We know nothing about you.'

Leah couldn't help her little laugh. Not hiding the curiosity, was she? 'What did you want to know?'

'Everything, of course.' The woman smiled back. 'Where did you meet Theo?'

'In London, a few months ago. It's been a whirlwind.'

The woman nodded. 'I'm not going to lie, we're all stunned. I never imagined he'd settle down. Certainly not so soon.'

Leah recognised the sharp questions in the woman's eyes but she gently shrugged and didn't reply. Theo was right: sometimes it was better to remain silent.

'Will you have lunch some time?' the woman invited.

'I'd like that very much, thank you.' Leah answered honestly, even though she knew the woman really just wanted to mine her for information. But she also knew the way to get people to soften up was to get them speaking. 'It's important to me to get to know Theo's world here in Athens and I'd love to see more of the city. What are some of your favourite spots?'

Having despatched his overly curious business acquaintance, Theo remained at a slight distance so he could watch her. Frankly he was still getting his head—and his libido—around her outfit. Her black trousers were nothing like her usual baggy jeans. These were silk and sleek, they sat ultra-low on her narrow waist and showed off the slim length of her legs. The scarlet blouse she had on top was almost sheer at the back, revealing a sweep of gleaming skin all the way down to the small of her back. The shirt hid that slight curve of her belly and he was glad people wouldn't realise she was pregnant. Not yet. He was still getting used to that idea himself.

Her hair was entwined somehow into a low twist at the nape of her neck. She had a touch of make-up on—something to make her eyes seem even bigger, brighter, and a slash of red lipstick that made her mouth irresistibly kissable.

He shouldn't have kissed her. Not because the world was watching, but because he wanted more. He wanted to *know* more too—what other secret dreams did she have? What other secret bold action did she want to take? This was the woman who'd thrown all caution to the wind that night with him. He'd been so privileged. He wanted her to feel that freedom with him again. He didn't know why the desire was this strong but he was sure they needed to get rid of it. He'd hoped it would dissipate, that he could ignore it…but he couldn't and he knew she couldn't either. It would be better to exhaust it. Then they could move forward with a calm, easy plan for the future. It didn't need to be a big deal.

And people *were* staring at her. She was so tall, so striking. So sexy. But also that mandatory engagement notice had run in the newspaper and everyone was agog. He'd laughed off the swirling rumours about his grandfather's quest to find him a suitable fiancée, but that he'd come back from London with a woman?

He couldn't help moving closer again—that protective urge rising even when he knew Leah didn't want it, or need it, given the apparent ease with which she was talking to Phoebe Mikos. But *he* needed it. He stood alongside her, listening as she asked more questions than she answered. She politely asked about places to see, things to do, intuitively making the most of these people's pride in their city, but she did it with an artless charm that made everyone around her smile.

'Do you mind if we leave, Leah?' he asked her eventually.

She turned to him and he saw the relief in her eyes. He drew her out and quietly directed his driver to take them to the Athens villa.

'You enjoyed yourself?' he asked as she stifled a yawn.

'It wasn't too bad,' she murmured. 'Your friends aren't so scary.'

'They're not all friends,' he couldn't help warning despite having seen her at ease there. The worry within him bloomed again.

'Competitors? Rivals? Threats?' She chuckled. 'None of those people could hurt you.'

'No?' Her certainty burned somehow. 'Do you think I don't feel anything?' he asked—even when he'd been the one trying to convince himself that he didn't. 'That I'm inhuman somehow?'

It was stupid to even ask. He'd been the one to tell her he couldn't love anyone—and that was true, wasn't it? It had to be.

She turned to face him. Her eyes were like deep pools and he just wanted to dive in.

'No. I know you've been hurt,' she breathed. 'I just don't know how.'

He rejected her words. But her vulnerability shone through—all that soft emotion pierced his own defence. He should say nothing but when she looked at him like that he couldn't help himself.

'They could hurt you,' he muttered.

'So it's me you're worried about?' She shook her head. 'I can let it wash over me.' Her frown formed as he said nothing. 'You don't believe me?'

'My mother struggled to break in here,' he confided huskily. 'Like you she wasn't Greek, she was American. They met on one of his trips away.' There'd been many trips away. 'She didn't speak the language. I didn't either until I came to live with Dimitri.' His father hadn't seen any need to teach him and his mother had been too absorbed with her own problems to bother to find him a tutor. 'He didn't bring either of us back to Greece. When he finally did, she came home most nights without him.'

He'd been ten years old when he'd discovered her drinking alone late at night, drowning that humiliation and loneliness from leaving his father at one of his all-night parties with all those other women. She'd screamed at Theo for disturbing her and sent him from the room. But he couldn't go back to bed. How could he sleep when the sound of her bitter sobs rang through the door she'd neglected to slam?

'They were miserable.' Leah sat very still. 'Did Dimitri know?'

'Dimitri lost his only child.' Theo too was frozen, his heart encased in the ice that had formed there so long ago. 'And he blamed my mother for everything.'

CHAPTER TEN

THEO SUDDENLY MOVED and Leah glanced out of the window, only just realising that the car had stopped outside a stunning building on the corner of an obviously exclusive part of downtown Athens. 'We're not going back to the compound?'

His eyes glittered in the darkness as he held the door for her. 'This is my city villa.'

Taken aback, Leah tried—and failed—not to be completely floored by the perfect façade of the historic villa.

'Is this where you slept the other night?' When she stepped inside, her heart stopped. Hard oak floors, and a marble staircase led up to more luxuriously styled furnishings. But here on the ground floor there was an internal decorative pool, of all things. The villa encapsulated a sense of peace that ought to have been impossible in the centre of such a vibrant city. She walked away from him, just to catch her breath. From this room there were incredible panoramic views of the Acropolis. Right now it was lit up, a beacon of ancient romantics. It was beyond beautiful but, inexplicably, anger welled within her.

'This is where you bring your women, so your grandfather doesn't see them,' she said with a laugh, but a curl of bitterness spiralled even as she tried to stop it. This was the scene of his secret seductions. All those beautiful women she'd seen tonight? Had any been his lover?

He had a whisker of a smile on his face. 'I don't wish to be disrespectful and—'

'You don't want to get his hopes up.'

His eyes were intent upon her as she gazed about the beautiful place.

'And you thought I'd want to stay here with you?'

'Leah,' he said softly. 'You're going to be my wife.' He crossed the small space between them. 'There hasn't been anyone in my bed since that night with you. I'm not and never have been promiscuous.'

The awful thing was, the nearer he got to her, the less she cared about those other women, whether they existed or not. They no longer mattered—she knew they'd meant little to him anyway. Because that was how he survived, wasn't it? With an impenetrable heart. Because he had been hurt. And it sounded as if his mother had been hurt too.

'Are you okay?' He frowned at her.

'I just…have a bit of a headache,' she muttered, stalling so she could try to think.

'Then let's get you a drink of water, shall we?'

She followed him into the kitchen. He leaned back against the counter, watching enigmatically as she sipped the iced water and briefly held the cold glass against her burning face.

'You should have been a model,' he suddenly said, his voice husky. 'You could have made millions.'

She laughed and put her glass down, her fingers stupidly shaky. 'Use my quirky features?'

'You must have considered it. Surely all tall, ultra-thin girls are approached at some point?'

'My parents forbade it.'

'Oh.' He grimaced. 'Of course they did.'

'I was supposed to make something of my brain, not my body.'

'So they wouldn't let you make the most of one of your assets.' He cocked his head. 'In fact, they made you feel…what? Ashamed of it somehow?'

She hated his insightfulness.

'And the other girls at school gave you grief?'

'They called me anorexic, of course. Then they saw how much I ate and assumed I must be bulimic. I'm just bony. It's the way I am.'

'I know.' He watched her. 'So your mother didn't like you wearing make-up or anything?'

'She refused to give money to an industry that thrives on insecurities.' She shrugged her shoulders. 'But you've seen her, she's the epitome of normal beauty ideals, right?'

He shook his head. 'We all like different things—'

'Don't be cute. You know what I mean. She's beautiful by anyone's standards. She doesn't need make-up or nice clothes to look amazing.'

'Nor do you. Nor does anyone.'

'But that doesn't mean they can't be fun. That doesn't mean you can't play with them and express yourself in all kinds of ways.' She'd just wanted to have a little fun.

'Usually you wear almost nothing but black—that's your self-expression?'

She shrugged. 'I gave in and just wore what's acceptable.'

'It doesn't matter how loose or dark you keep your clothing, you can't actually hide, Leah. You're not and never will be invisible.'

Yet almost all her life she'd wanted to be. Ironically, the only time she'd felt free of performance pressure was when she was onstage.

'Not tonight at least, no.' She smiled down at her blouse. 'Is this your way of saying you like it?'

'You should wear whatever you want to wear. Be the shadow, be the sunlight, be whatever you want. Just be yourself in that moment. There is no right or wrong.'

She smiled at him.

Something unfathomable flickered in his eyes. 'Why did you say yes to me that night?'

'Why?' She was stunned he'd need to ask. 'Your ego needs a stroke?'

'No, I really want to understand. Why me? Why that one night? Why not some other guy, some other time?'

'There was no other guy. No other time.'

'I don't believe you.'

She stared at him. 'Um…have you forgotten you were my first?'

'Oh, I'll never forget that,' he purred. 'But I think you had other chances before me. Maybe you just didn't notice them.'

'That's very kind of you. But no.' She shook her head.

'Liar.'

She stared at him, then glanced away. 'Okay, there was one guy who asked me out. But he didn't want *me*, he wanted to get on my mother's research team.'

'He tried to use you to get close to your parents?'

She nodded. 'I was working in their laboratory as an assistant. Because I didn't finish my degree.' Because she'd failed in their eyes.

'Because you never wanted to actually *do* the degree.'

'The things we try to do to please our parents, right?' she murmured. 'Like you marrying me to please your grandfather.'

'That's not the same,' he scoffed.

'Isn't it?'

'Nobody held a gun to my head to make me take you to bed,' he said. 'That desire is very real. It's *still* very real.'

She didn't reply; she couldn't.

'So did you date him?' he prompted her.

She shuddered to even think of it. 'We went out for about a month.'

'And you didn't sleep with him?' His eyebrows arched.

'One month isn't that long—'

'You weren't into him.'

Shocked, she laughed. 'No, he wasn't really into me.'

'No, he would have been. *You* didn't let him close.'

She paused.

'If you'd really been attracted to him you would have. You slept with me, a total stranger you met that very night.'

Um, that had been *so* different.

He chuckled. 'Come on, Leah. Aren't I just a little bit right? That other guy didn't turn you on and there was no other chance because you never let there be one. You buried yourself away in a laboratory with a bunch of guys too shy to see past their microscopes.'

'Don't stereotype them.' She mock-punched him.

'I bet it's true. And then you go work with a bunch of old people? You say you don't want to be invisible but you have been hiding, Leah.' He stepped closer. 'Maybe you only picked me because you found out I was leaving the very next day. In that way, I was safe.'

'You were a total stranger—how safe was that? It was an insane risk to go off with you.'

'Is that why you said yes to me, Leah?' He

leaned closer. 'Because you thought I couldn't hurt you?'

She hadn't thought anything of the sort. She hadn't thought at all. 'I said yes because I couldn't say no to you. You're irresistible, okay?' She folded her arms across her chest.

'So are you.'

She shook her head.

'They killed your self-confidence.' He reached for her. 'That shouldn't have happened—'

'How was I supposed to stop them?' she flung back, broken. 'All my life, Theo...my grades weren't good enough. I'm too tall. Too angular. Too different... Nobody wants to get hurt, Theo. You don't either.' She pushed back. 'In fact, you work stupidly hard to protect people *you* feel responsible for. Not only do you not want to get hurt, you don't want anyone around you to get hurt either.'

He lifted his chin, his gaze sharpening.

'What developed that over-protectiveness, Theo? Who did you see get hurt?' She waited but then continued boldly. 'It's not your grandfather. He's strong. He's a powerful man who's only recently become vulnerable. This goes back further than that. Who *couldn't* you help? Was it your mum?'

'I'm not over-protective. The truth is I have no desire to have to protect anyone.'

'Not even people you care about? Or is it that you don't want to care about people *because* you were hurt?' She paused. 'Why did you go to live with Dimitri? What happened to her?'

Theo sighed and turned away from her. This evening was not going the way he'd envisaged. He'd rather hoped they'd be on to round two by now; but somehow he'd ended up bringing up things he shouldn't have in the car on the drive back and now she wanted to know more.

'Just tell me, Theo,' she muttered. 'You can tell me anything. I won't judge.'

He never talked to anyone about this. And there was such a risk if he told her the truth. But he didn't want to brush off her concern. He knew he had to explain even just a little of it— so she'd understand why it was he couldn't give her everything she ought to have. He owed her that. 'They had a blazing affair that led to a shot-gun marriage.'

Shock, then consternation pinched her face. 'Your mother got pregnant?'

'With me. Yes.'

She swallowed. 'And you're an only child.'

'Correct.'

Her colour receded. He knew she was picturing their future, drawing the parallels to his past. He didn't blame her—he'd done the same.

'They were miserable.' He forced himself to continue with the sorry story and finish it as briefly as he could. He didn't want her taking it on board or reading anything into it. He never talked about it because it didn't matter, it didn't mean anything. It was in the past and could stay there. She never needed to know the whole of it. 'The sizzle fizzled pretty quickly. It became a mess of fights and infidelity.' He didn't go deeper into details. 'After my father died in a car accident my mother decided she couldn't give me the best life so she sent me to live with Dimitri.' He breathed out. 'I'm not going to repeat those past mistakes, Leah. We won't be unhappy like that.'

She was silent for a long moment. 'This is why you came up with your prison island plan?'

'It seemed like a good idea,' he muttered. She didn't realise what that island meant to him but, of course, what was a heaven to him might be a hell for her. He couldn't make assumptions on her behalf any more. 'But we'll work something else out if you'd prefer.'

Her eyes widened. 'You're not going to send me away the second we're married?'

'No.'

Relief unfurled at his words, tempered by the sad history he'd just told her. No wonder he'd thought separation from the start was for the best. It sounded as though his parents' marriage had been a mess. Leah's heart ached. She desperately wanted to know more, but his expression had shuttered and she knew he'd hated having even this brief discussion about it. He was reserved—as private as he was protective—and she could respect that even though really she just wanted to reach out and touch him and tell him she was sorry for what he'd been through. Maybe she had to handle this with the same emotional restraint that he was. Because this 'sizzle would fizzle', wouldn't it?

Her heart puckered at the prospect. She couldn't imagine not wanting to be near to him. But at least she knew he wasn't going to be unfaithful—not when he'd been this scarred. She tried to push past it, to get them both back on an easier track. She'd focus on the practicalities of their immediate future.

'Do we have to marry at the town hall or something?' Would there be a bunch of strangers staring at them as they waited in a crowded hall outside before their five-minute service?

He shook his head. 'I've secured permission for us to marry on the compound.'

'So there won't be many people?'

'Dimitri will be there. My security team…' He paused, as if realising how impersonal it all sounded. 'I'm sorry your family are unable to attend.'

'I'm sorry Oliver can't make it, but it'll be more fun without my parents.' Honestly, she was brightened by the news she wasn't going to have to parade in front of people she didn't know. 'We could get married in our pyjamas before breakfast,' she said, shooting him a kittenish smile to ease the tension.

'Dimitri wouldn't approve.'

'Well, we mustn't disappoint him.' She chuckled. 'After all, this is only about pleasing your grandfather.'

'Oh, snarky Leah is back, your headache must be better.' But a rueful smile had lightened his features as she'd laughed. 'Do you have something to wear?'

'You just said there aren't going to be many people there,' she said limpidly.

'*I'm* going to be there,' he gasped, mock-wounded.

'That's good, I guess,' she pondered with

thoughtful pretence, enjoying this turn back towards the easy banter with that bite of desire beneath. She loved it when he eased up on his solemnity and she wanted to wipe away the remnants of that old hurt in his eyes. In this very immediate future, she could touch him on this most literal of levels. 'It's the only time you'll ever see me in a dress.'

'Do you hate your legs or something?' His smile turned sly and he stepped forward to tug at her scarlet blouse. 'You have no idea how good they feel locked around me.'

The awkwardness melted inside her. Why did it take only this? Only a smile and a look and a touch and she was cast back towards him, happily seeking more of his caresses. 'Theo—'

'They're gorgeously long and stronger than they look.' He glanced down and then swiftly lifted his lashes to imprison her in his heated green gaze. 'I get so turned on when you have me in your grip.'

'Like I'm some spider?' She playfully ducked his reach for her, but was breathless beneath it.

He laughed. 'Stop trying to avoid my compliments.'

'Oh, you were complimenting me? I thought you were telling me my legs are like…tweezers or something while trying to maul me at the same time.'

'Maul you?' His laugh morphed into a sexy growl and he planted firm hands on her hips, keeping her right where she wanted to be. 'You want me to show you again?'

'Show me what?' She couldn't resist leaning into him, giving up on any idea of escape.

'What we're really good at.'

She'd wanted this again so much, for so long. She couldn't possibly say no.

He drew her closer and that look in his eyes intensified. 'Let me touch you.'

She loved that he asked, even when he knew her answer. And even when she knew he meant only this, only now, she lifted her chin. He met her parted mouth with his in a kiss so hot, so desperately needed she moaned helplessly. Her eyes closed as she was thrown instantly back into that delicious firestorm of delight and desire.

'Your legs are the perfect length for me too...' he teased between kisses. 'If only you had some heels on, even just a couple of inches.'

'I can't wear heels,' she gasped, on one last joke. 'I'd trip over.'

He caught her laugh with a kiss. 'You're graceful as hell and you know it. Anyway, you wouldn't need to walk, you could just brace against the wall. You'd be the perfect height for me. Otherwise I'd have to bend and get muscle burn.'

She huffed another breathless laugh. 'Always thinking of the practicalities?'

'We'd be able to sustain it for longer.'

She couldn't sustain herself for long at all around him, and the prospect of hot sex against the wall made her knees buckle.

His laugh was an exultant sexy sound but she didn't care. All that mattered was that he'd slid his arm beneath her and scooped her up. He climbed the stairs, effortlessly carrying her to a vast bedroom. She couldn't look away from him as he set her in the centre of the bed. His eyes glazed as his focus dropped and he looked down her body. That rapt, fixated look made her toes curl. And then it began. Pure attraction, pure pleasure flowed as he stripped them both bare with lingering caresses. But her desire was underpinned by that other ache—that need for touch that was more than physical—and that made her feel everything so very much more. She sobbed, her emotion unstoppable in that moment when he thrust within her again. At last.

'Theo—' she cried out at the culmination of relief and craving.

'I'm here.'

Yes.

CHAPTER ELEVEN

'THEO HAS LEFT for work already.' Leah smiled apologetically as she poured Dimitri a cup of tea as he joined her at the table on the terrace. Since that conversation when she'd asked him to help her, Dimitri had thawed—coaching her in beginner Greek phrases and instructing Amalia to do the same. The week had passed with increasing ease and speed. Theo had returned her to the compound early the morning after the exhibition and Amalia had swung into action to help her with preparations. She'd enlisted her cousin and aunt as well because they were so low on time.

This morning the sun warmed Leah's back as she resumed knitting the white silk as quickly and as neatly as she could. Amalia was already working on her section too. Theo had left well over an hour ago.

'He works too hard.' Dimitri stirred his tea.

'Perhaps he will work less now there is a child coming.'

'Perhaps.' Leah didn't hold out much hope but she'd heard the wistful tinge to the older man's words and she didn't want to lie to him.

Dimitri studied her with his faded version of Theo's bright green eyes. His held more blue and weren't as vivid yet he still seemed to see right through her.

'He's not perfect,' Dimitri said.

'No one is.' She smiled, unsure where he was going with this but she wasn't going to say a word against Theo to his grandfather.

'I was too hard on him.'

For a moment she held Dimitri's gaze, recognising that hint of arrogance in the way he held his head. But then he dropped his chin and his shoulders sagged.

'I didn't want him to become like his father, but Theo was always different...' The old man coughed. 'He's loyal. He cares deeply...'

Leah stared at him, realising how hard it was for him to say any of this.

'He loves you very much. He doesn't want to let you down,' she said.

'I know. Because of that, he works too hard.'

He gazed across the pool. 'Perhaps now he has you, that will change.'

Dimitri had been a workaholic as well. The discipline in his daily routine proved that. While routine could provide a safe structure and enable achievement, it could also reinforce bad habits. Strengths were also weaknesses, sometimes, and working too hard for too long could definitely become a weakness.

She smiled to hide her thoughts. 'Theo and I understand each other. We respect each other.'

'But you don't love each other.'

Her skin cindered with embarrassment. She respected Theo. She'd be loyal to him and she was insanely attracted to him. Anything more than that, she couldn't bear to consider.

'Perhaps that is good.' He picked up his coffee. 'Marrying for suitability rather than love works better in the long term.' He nodded. 'He is different from his father.'

So his father had married for love? Or what he'd thought at the time had been love. Theo had called it a 'blazing affair' that had led to an unplanned pregnancy. She and he hadn't had the affair. They'd had only the one night. Though they'd had a couple more since.

'Is he different from you?' Leah asked, curious

enough to push past her nerves. 'Did you marry for love or was it merely a suitable arrangement?'

'It began as one and became another. That is what happens.'

'A suitable arrangement grew into love?' she asked.

'As it will for you.'

Of course he wanted to believe that. He loved Theo and he didn't want what had happened to his son to happen to his grandson.

'You don't think the same can happen in reverse?' she asked warily. 'An unsuitable love match can't become suitable?'

Dimitri's expression shut down. 'No.'

Wild love—wild *lust*—didn't last. She suspected Theo thought they were burning out the lust between them, then it would become a convenient arrangement somehow. But for her, the intensity hadn't lessened. It was worsening.

Because it's not just lust.

She closed her mind to that awful whisper and poured both herself and Dimitri some fresh orange juice. She'd focus on finishing her dress and learning Greek.

Theo returned every night to the riviera compound, unable to spend another night away from her. He'd carve out their new normal after the wedding, but right now the temptation to return to her was extreme. And he couldn't resist it. He couldn't resist the need to touch her. But his discomfort was growing. He couldn't seem to think as clearly. He found himself distracted at work—wondering what she was doing. It was unacceptable.

He knew some distance was required.

Tonight he roved through the house but knew she'd be on the terrace. She liked the sunset. He heard her laughter as he neared. He walked faster but quietly, surprised by the sound of other voices, others laughing.

He paused in the open doorway. Leah sat at the table, her back to him. She looked vibrant in loose white linen trousers and a clingy blue shirt. Amalia was with her and so was Dimitri. They were laughing together. He didn't think he'd ever seen Dimitri laugh like that. She didn't notice him for a while. They were sampling a se-lection of traditional sweet cakes.

'Leah likes the lemon.' Dimitri noticed him first and sat back with a satisfied twinkle in his eye as he called to him. 'She has good taste.'

Theo stared as Leah smiled and coyly thanked Dimitri in Greek. She had a private joke going with his grandfather? Since when did they begin talking like this? Since when did his grandfather joke?

Theo shook his head and pulled out a chair to join them, trying to shift the uneasy weight pressing down on his chest. 'Preferring the lemon over the plum?'

Her eyes sparkled as she smiled again at his grandfather. His gut tightened and his appetite vanished. He didn't want dinner. He didn't want to sit here and watch them all laughing together. He wanted her alone, in his bed, her attention all on him.

He stilled, stunned at his own rabid—*jealousy*?

He should have known what damn sweet she liked. *He* should have sought it out for her. His grandfather seemed to know more about her than he did. His staff too…

And whose fault is that?

He'd been determined to work as much as he could this week. Determined to do this right so he didn't ruin her life completely. He refused to let her become miserable. But suddenly he wasn't sure what was right any more.

His island idea had definitely been wrong. He'd not understood her need for companionship or to feel valued, visible in her role as his fiancée.

And now, he didn't like the thought of her being so far away. Even a thirty-minute flight time felt too long.

He couldn't understand why he couldn't keep this simple. Why did he suddenly want things he'd never wanted before in his life? Never had he ached to leave work early the way he did now knowing she was here.

He somehow got through supper, listening to them talking and laughing, watching Leah at ease—chatting, funny, kind. It was late when Amalia walked Dimitri back to his building, leaving Theo alone with Leah at last.

'You came home earlier tonight.' She broke the silence with her soft voice.

He nodded, unable to take his eyes off her.

'Are you going to work tomorrow morning?' Her chin lifted.

'Yes.' He leaned back in his seat and tried to ignore the slight pout of her lower lip. 'I figured it gives me something to fill in the time before the ceremony.'

She put down her spoon. 'What happens after? You go back to work?'

'No,' he answered mildly, despite the tension stringing him out. 'We go on our honeymoon.'

'To prison island?' Her lashes lowered, hiding her eyes.

'It's a surprise.' To his astonishment he actually felt a little nervous about it.

The feeling compelled him to silence her next question in the best way possible. He couldn't resist any longer anyway. He stalked around the table and kissed her till she was breathless. He ached to pull her to her feet and hustle her inside so he could have her in his bed. Restraint was imperative yet apparently impossible. Rebellion at his self-imposed restrictions bubbled his blood. He couldn't stand the need and the want clawing within him. Since when did he want anything with this intensity?

'I'm not sleeping with you tonight,' he said huskily. 'It's the eve of our wedding, it'd be bad luck.'

'Well, we wouldn't want any more of *that*.' Something flashed in her eyes.

His breath stalled in his lungs. 'That's how you feel? That this was unlucky?'

She put her hand on her belly. 'No,' she whispered. 'I don't think that about this. It's a miracle in a way…coming into being…against all odds, right?'

He still didn't want to think about the child. Instead he kissed her again until every nerve tingled.

'No,' he muttered with a low groan as he pulled away from her. 'Not tonight.'

He watched the dazedness in her eyes dissipate as disappointment loomed. His gut ached. He hated disappointing her. Which was exactly why he needed to prove his restraint now and build distance back again over the coming days.

'I'll see you tomorrow, Leah,' he said huskily.

When she'd become his wife.

He went to work in the morning purely to put himself beyond temptation. But he got no actual work achieved. He spent a couple of hours pacing while talking on the phone, finalising the arrangements for their travel later in the day. The idea had come to him when he'd been unable to sleep a couple of nights ago and he'd been unable to resist putting it in play.

He returned to the compound in time to shower. His tailor had delivered the new suit and shirt. His shoes were new too. Everything was new. Except him. He was still the same—with the same failings. She had no idea really. Tension tightened his muscles as he dressed. He'd consider this a contractual meeting like any other, right? Just another merger.

But he'd never wanted to make promises like this to someone. Not these deeply personal promises he knew he could never keep.

Fidelity—fine. Honour—fine. To love?

Leah was sweet. And she was having a *child*. He breathed out, refusing to undo the top button of the stiff shirt that suddenly strangled him.

He turned his back on his reflection and strode outside. Dimitri was sitting out on the terrace. Amalia was also there with her husband and their son. Leah had insisted they attend as guests, not staff. He was glad she'd charmed them. It shouldn't have surprised him; when anyone got to know Leah, they discovered her sweet generosity.

They'd had a shade put over the pergola to protect them from the stunning blue sky and the heat of the sun. Tendrils of white flowers and greenery had been wound around the pillars and made the compound even more picturesque than usual. His security team had swept the beach and ensured there was no one with any cameras and long-range lenses hiding out. They had complete privacy. He'd called in Philip, his security chief, as his witness. The official from the city arrived and briefly ran over the paperwork with him. All that remained was for his bride to appear. He stared down at his watch. Would she keep him waiting? His breathing shallowed. Suddenly it seemed imperative—he *needed* to see her right now.

The official coughed discreetly and Theo looked up.

His throat tightened. She was a column of white and silver—gleaming like a pale angel with a smile that was both pure and a little playful. The tiny sparkle of confidence felled him. She walked towards him. The white flowers that she held low covered that gentle curve of her belly. A lace shawl covered her shoulders. A white bodice—was it knitted?—hugged her hips and flared from there in a cloud of soft tulle— a subtle reminder of the softness to be found in her straight slenderness. It was all he could do to hold himself upright. He couldn't wait to slip her out of it. He couldn't look at her but he couldn't tear his gaze away. It was like being strung on a medieval torture device. The official stood in front of them, alternately speaking in Greek, then English, so his bride understood. Theo braced, forcing himself to stop staring at her like a crazy man—to take in the ceremony and actually speak when required.

A quick glance behind her showed his grandfather sitting in a chair, leaning forward on his walking stick. A week ago Theo would've expected the old man would be prune-faced, given she wasn't one of his picks, but he was actually smiling and relaxed. He genuinely liked her.

Theo looked at Leah again. Something ached within him. He didn't want to hurt her and he would. It was in his DNA.

The official was beaming and looking at him expectantly. She was looking at him too—too trusting, too wary, too wanting. That panic—to protect her—surged within him. But he was supposed to kiss her now. He bent forward and brushed his lips over hers in the briefest of touches. He couldn't allow himself anything more or he'd lose all control.

At last it was over. They were married.

'Are you sorry your family isn't here?' His voice was hoarse as he walked with her to pose for a photo.

She shook her head. 'No.'

But there was a yearning look within her eyes that smote his heart. He steeled himself against it.

'Your dress…' He struggled to push the words past the tightening in his throat. 'You made it.'

She bit her lip, glancing down. 'Yes.'

'How did you have the time?' He couldn't fathom it. It was so intricate and beautiful, it had to have taken hours.

'Amalia and her family helped. They knitted around the clock once they saw the design.'

His heart seemed to stop. 'Who designed it?'

'I did. I adapted an idea I'd been working on.'

He nodded and looked down and that was when he saw her shoes. His mouth felt as if wads of cotton wool had been stuffed into it. He couldn't swallow or speak. He could only stare and then try like hell to control the desire coursing through his body—but it was as if the sluices at an ancient dam had been unlocked.

They were silver shoes, dainty, with delicious little high heels.

And they were for him. He appreciated the gesture more than he'd imagined he could appreciate anything. Touched a part of him so deeply buried he'd not known it was there. All he wanted to do was touch her.

He ached to rid himself of this desperate need. Why hadn't it eased over these past few days? Why wasn't it settling now that he had her safety and security ensured? He had everything working in play just as he wanted it. Yet his tension was now worse than ever.

Leah stared up at Theo, watching the storminess build in his emerald eyes. He was so silent, so inscrutable. She swallowed. 'You don't like it?'

'Like what?' he muttered, blinking as if he'd lost track of the conversation.

Embarrassment curled within her. 'My dress.'

She shouldn't have made it. Should have just bought one of those amazing designer numbers in central Athens. It had taken so many hours, so much planning. She'd had so much companionship with Amalia.

Theo's expression sharpened and he opened his mouth.

'Theo, Leah,' Amalia called to them, breaking the spell.

Leah glanced; the photographer wanted another photo. Theo put his arm around her waist and pulled her closer. He did it with such speed, she was almost tipped off balance. Leah glanced up at him to read his expression, given the tension she could feel within him. But he'd looked to the lens. He wasn't smiling.

'Perfect,' the man said.

Theo released her waist but immediately took her hand in his and led her to the table. It was laden with a selection of delicacies—a celebratory feast Leah could barely touch. Theo didn't each much either.

'Traditions are important,' Dimitri said stiffly. 'It might be a small wedding but it is important to do things properly.'

She felt Theo's tension magnify as they were called to cut the beautiful cake.

They sliced into the cake together and, once everyone had a small piece, Dimitri made a toast to them.

Leah nibbled at the cake, stupidly nervous, which was crazy given she was no wedding-night virgin. She *knew* Theo. Yet at the same time she didn't. Right now she couldn't figure out what he was thinking, only that it was apparently unpleasant. Her heart sank; he really hadn't wanted to do this. The intimacy she'd thought they'd built over the last few days was nothing.

'Leah and I need to get going now,' he said to Dimitri.

The old man replied in Greek. Theo smiled

and Dimitri, Amalia and the others melted away with teasing smiles.

But Theo dropped his polite smile as he walked towards her.

'Should I go get changed?' she asked him anxiously. She didn't know what he had planned.

'No,' he snapped grimly. 'We need to leave right away.'

CHAPTER TWELVE

SHE WAS ALMOST afraid to speak, his expression was that severe as he led her to the helipad. But she refused to be afraid of her husband. 'So it's not prison island?' she attempted a joke.

'No.' He waited for her to climb into the helicopter ahead of him.

So now they were en route to who knew where. He helped her with the headset and she then watched out of the window as they took off. The view over the mainland was just stunning—she drank in the blue waters and stunning settlements. Then they seemed to lower and slow a little. She leaned forward, gazing intently as ancient ruins came more sharply into view. Ruins she recognised because she'd studied them online a few thousand times years ago when caught up in the romance of the novel she'd loved.

'Is that Delphi?' She turned to him, her heart thudding because she knew it was. 'You *remembered.*' And she was so touched.

'I remember everything about that night,' he muttered—all soft, serious intensity.

She couldn't turn away from him—he was so still, as if he was struggling to contain something. The tension between them tightened. 'Thank you.'

'Go on,' he ordered roughly. 'Look.'

She turned towards the window again as they circled the site. The setting sun cast a burning glow on the ancient hewn stone. It was majestic and so moving. She knew Theo had timed their trip to perfection so she had this magical view—this was why he'd insisted they leave the compound so suddenly. Her vision misted at his thoughtfulness.

They circled the ancient ruins one last time and then headed away from the mountains, passing over the terracotta roofs of a village below. It was so picturesque, with narrow cobbled streets that she could see even from this height. Eventually the chopper lowered to a secluded property on the far outskirts of the village.

As she stood back on the ground Leah paused, conscious of her appearance as the helicopter lifted up and away. She glanced about anxiously, expecting an assistant to appear to carry their luggage in, but no one emerged from the magnificent building.

'The staff left about five minutes ago,' Theo said, lifting the two overnight bags himself. 'So we're alone.'

She followed him from the helipad along the pathway until they turned a hedged corner into the private heart of the property. She paused near the edge of the pool and took in the inviting atmosphere. There was soft music playing from discreet speakers. Candles burned in glass jars placed in carefully chosen spots. The small circles of flickering light cast a warm glow around the terrace, almost creating a semi-circular stage.

'The American half of me wants my first dance.' Theo dropped the bags and faced her. That rough edge to his voice was even grittier.

She swallowed, realising that he was holding something fierce back. 'Theo—'

'I apologise for the lack of a live band.' He slowly paced towards her. 'But I wanted us to be alone.'

'Why?'

'I'm a terrible dancer.' He held out his hand and his smile was tight.

'I don't believe you.'

He wasn't terrible at anything. But she put her

hand in his and he drew her into that little lit space on the terrace.

'I don't know how I've resisted touching you all day.' He pulled her into his arms. 'I can't resist any more. You look beautiful.' He stared into her eyes.

That warmth within trickled more quickly, more deeply—becoming a heat that needed release.

'And you're wearing heels,' he noted.

'I figured it wouldn't matter if I fell over when it was only you watching.'

'Only me?' He cocked his head and finally his smile appeared.

It was unfair of him to flirt with her when he didn't really mean it. And the truth was she was likely to tumble *because* it was him. He put her so on edge, so aware of every movement, every breath when she was with him, yet not with him. Now she simply ached for his touch.

'This lace thing is pretty, but I'm afraid I'm going to tear it if I hold you closer.'

'I wore it to cover my shoulders...' she muttered breathlessly. 'And to hide the fact that...'

'That what?'

'I'm not wearing anything beneath the dress.'

She swallowed. 'I tried but you could see the lines…'

He inhaled deeply. 'So you're telling me that beneath this angelic surface, there's a temptress. I think I knew that.' He pulled her hips against his and she felt just how much he liked how she looked. 'I remember those scarlet panties,' he whispered.

'Good thing there's no audience,' she said with a chuckle.

'Right now I wouldn't give a damn if there was.' His breathing roughened. 'I can't wait any more, Leah.'

That twisting serpent of heat bit her too. She threw herself into the gorgeous escape of this— their touch, in the magic they created together. Hot and dream-like, the searing need enveloped her. They were moving, but not really dancing. Somehow she was back against the wall of the building and she gasped as he plundered, kissing his way down her neck. She threw her head back to let him and glimpsed the darkening sky above and saw the stars emerging. His fingers moved and the silver strap slipped off her shoulder in the haste and the front of her dress dropped enough to bare her breast.

He stared, savage hunger etched on his face. 'Leah.'

She shivered as his fingers teased in gentle swirling motions that only made her fire flare. She needed him. Now.

'I don't know how to get you out of this dress fast enough without damaging it,' he groaned.

She'd laugh if she weren't so desperate. 'Then don't.'

Looking into her eyes, he moved, freeing himself with the simple slide of a zip, and then he lifted the skirt of her dress and pressed close, nudging her legs further apart with his.

'You wore the shoes for me,' he muttered roughly, 'so we could do this.'

She felt a flash of vulnerability—a sudden fear that the effort she'd gone to revealed something more, something she hadn't wanted him to see. But there was no time to fret as he took her hands in his, palm to palm, and laced their fingers. She gasped, anticipation soaring as he braced them on the wall either side of her head.

There was this between them. *This.* Powerful. Primitive. Unsophisticated. Undeniable. The simplest, most basic of needs. The drive to get closer to him pushed her to arch her hips forward as her shoulders pressed against the wall.

But not only were her hands locked in his, her gaze was locked in the fierceness of his focus too. Neither smiled; it was impossible in this supreme intensity. She felt him, close and hard and almost hers. Hunger and passion forced her to rock, sliding closer still. And he was right there.

'See?' he gritted, almost smiled, but the tension was too strong. 'Perfect.'

He watched her as he thrust. Her scream echoed through the night. But he didn't stop. He possessed her—physically and beyond as his gaze seared through to her soul and she met him arch for thrust, in a frantic, fast ride that was so explosive, so powerful it could end only one way. In an almost instant eruption of blinding, white-hot pleasure.

And then there was silence. They were still completely dressed. Still desperately entwined—their fine clothes tangled. But her emotions were torn—because that had been so much more than *simple*. The sheer desperation, the total annihilation stunned her. As did the deeper, complex yearning it revealed.

'What a first dance,' she mumbled, seeking a way to claw some lightness back into the atmosphere because it was so intense that she couldn't breathe.

She carried her pretty, heeled shoes in one hand while her husband held her other hand tightly, leading her through the silent villa up the stairs to the moonlit room. She faced him and felt that desire ricochet back. Because they were so far from done.

'Slower this time, Leah.' He carefully slipped the wrap and the dress from her body and placed them over a chair reverently.

He glanced at her, then practically tore his trousers and shirt off with such fierce speed she chuckled. But then he stepped forward and she couldn't laugh any more and he made true on his promise. It was slow. It was thorough. And it destroyed her.

Long fingers of sunlight slid up the bed, slowly warming and waking her. She felt Theo's arms around her and smiled secretly. He must have sensed her waken because he began gently tracing patterns on her back.

'You're not leaving right away to go to work?' she asked sleepily.

'Leah,' he admonished piously. 'It's our honeymoon.'

'As if that minor fact would stop you.' She smiled and kept her eyes closed.

'Did you wake up on the wrong side of the

bed? Or just not get enough sleep last night, darling?' He pressed a kiss to her shoulder and slid out of bed.

She didn't want to get out of bed ever. She wanted him to get back into it. And he knew. But he didn't come back to her; instead he picked up her dress from where he'd placed it and carefully put it on a hanger. 'Thank you.'

'It's stunning.' He picked up the accompanying lace, which had fallen by her side of the bed. 'Did Amalia loan you this?'

Surprised, she reached out and ran her fingertip over the delicate lace. 'No, Dimitri gave that to me. You didn't realise?'

'Realise what?'

'He said his wife made it. She wore it on their wedding day.'

He stared at the lacework in his hands. 'And he gave it to you?' His lips twisted into a rueful smile. 'You've won him over completely.'

'It's because I'm carrying the next Savas.'

'No, it's because he likes you. You're patient with him—I've seen you pouring his tea and plumping his pillows.'

'He's an old man, Theo. Of course I'm patient and it's not hard to be kind.'

'You're patient with everyone. You do things

for people.' He drew in a deep breath. 'And you're talented. You made the blanket you gave that woman at the home. Your cardigan you wore that night at the ballet...'

She nodded.

'I saw the drawings in your apartment. They were on graph paper.'

'I work up the patterns, yes.'

'You learned some maths then, back with your parents' insistence.' He grinned.

'I wasn't bad at it, I just wasn't good enough by their impossible standards. I'd be sent to my room to study and end up knitting to help me relax,' she acknowledged. 'I made leg warmers for my ballet class. Awful stripes from ugly left-over balls of wool that were cheap. Zoe wore hers to company class the other week and a friend wanted some.'

'You could sell them.'

'They take a while for me to knit. They can buy machine-made ones for cheaper.'

'So you've thought about it.' He sat beside her. 'Yours are artisan creations. Hand-crafted, beautiful wool—a premium product.'

She shook her head and giggled at the flattery. 'Hardly. I make mistakes. I can't put a massive price tag on imperfect pieces.'

'Handmade doesn't have to mean perfect.' He looked thoughtful. 'You could sell the patterns. People would then knit them themselves.'

She hesitated, half tempted by his idea. 'You think they're that good?'

'Don't you?' He turned her face up when she glanced down. 'Don't you believe in yourself, Leah?'

She swallowed again.

'Because you should. Just because you didn't get top in every damn math or physics class doesn't mean you're not capable of amazing things. It's just different.'

'I know that. I know.'

'There's a difference between knowing and *believing*.'

He stole her breath with his words. Then he kissed her and stole everything else she had to give.

A blissful hour later he nudged her with a smile. 'Let's go exploring.'

She wasn't sure she'd ever be able to move again. But she let him tug her to her feet and followed him into the shower. Theo drove them to Delphi, where they spent the afternoon exploring the ruins.

'This is incredible.' The beauty of her surroundings amazed her but at the same time she was keenly aware of the strong man walking beside her. 'Thank you.' She glanced towards him, only her gaze ensnared with his. 'You're supposed to be seeing the sights.'

'I am.'

She rolled her eyes, but when she swallowed it was hard to push past the lump that had formed there. This was so lovely, it scared her. He took the lead, turning into the most knowledgeable tour guide ever, telling her anecdotes about the area, pointing out all kinds of features.

'I read up yesterday morning,' he explained as she looked at him in disbelief over one obscure fact.

'I thought you were working.'

'I couldn't concentrate.'

Theo couldn't resist holding her hand as they turned to walk back down the hillside. When he'd watched her at the ballet she'd been like this—the expressive emotions flickering on her face. There was nothing better than seeing her entranced. Smiling. Moved. He liked it best of all when she was moved by him—by his touch. In bed—vulnerable and exposed.

'Do you need to check in with Dimitri?' she asked as they walked back towards the car.

She really cared for the old man. He glanced at her and knew she was genuine. She was good at building relationships—she had an easier relationship with Dimitri than Theo had ever had. Which was remarkable given her own family dynamics. 'What about you checking in with your family?'

'I did. My brother sent a message back yesterday morning,' she said happily. 'He actually remembered.'

Smiling, Theo phoned Dimitri, who immediately asked to speak to Leah. With dutiful mockery, he passed his phone to her and watched as she shyly said hello in Greek. It was only a couple of moments before she ended the call.

'I think he likes you more than me,' Theo teased as he drove them back to the private villa.

She grinned and looked at him. 'You're the CEO of his business, Theo. That's after adding to the conglomerate. You've done everything he's ever asked of you. More than everything.'

'He expected nothing but the best.' He stilled.

'And you've always delivered.' She angled her head. 'But what do you want for yourself, Theo? I have my outlet—what's yours?' She leaned close. 'Please don't say it's having one-night stands with women in London...'

He couldn't smile. 'I have my work. I like my work.'

'Is that enough?'

What else was there? He got into the car and waited for her to fasten her seat belt before driving off. 'I was young when I went to live with Dimitri,' he said. 'He was a tough taskmaster, but it was a good distraction.'

'And that's it? You just work? I thought the adage was work hard, *play* hard...'

'I don't feel my life is boring, Leah.' It certainly wasn't any more. Not with her in it.

But he felt her gaze on him, too searching, too soft.

'You take it upon yourself to ensure Dimitri's happiness—by pleasing him.'

'Like you've never tried to please anyone?' He forced a laugh. 'You make that your life's work.'

'We both had expectations placed on us—the difference is I failed all mine. But you surpassed them—awards, accolades, grades, prizes, acquisitions, business acumen...and you've been perfect ever since,' she muttered.

'I have been so far from perfect, Leah.' He grimaced. He didn't want her feeling sorry for him; it was preposterous. 'No one is perfect.'

'Were you afraid he'd send you away too?'

Suddenly it was as if all the oxygen had been sucked from the car.

'Is that what happened?' she asked softly. 'Did your mother send you away?'

He kept his eyes on the road and pressed harder on the accelerator. He didn't talk about that— ever.

'Why did she let you go?' Leah was so calm and soft and insistent and somehow…safe.

It was the question he'd spent most of his life asking and he still didn't know the answer. All he knew was that it hurt. It would always hurt. He just never admitted it. He never let it get this personal with anyone. But Leah disarmed him with her self-deprecating lovely laugh that made him smile. She was so gorgeously human and he truly couldn't resist confessing it to her.

'She said it would be better for me to be with the Savas family. That she couldn't look after me properly any more.' He sighed. 'She'd started drinking and only drank more as their marriage fell apart.' He cleared his throat. 'Don't think badly of her.'

Leah shook her head slightly.

'My father was Dimitri's golden boy. He was their only child and I guess he had a lot of pressure on him. But he was also spoilt and selfish and partied hard. And I guess it was partly rebellion that made him marry the girl he'd got pregnant and move to the States with her.' He tensed. 'He was unfaithful from the start. My mother kept me informed—justifying her own indiscretions, her own addictions. But I didn't need her to tell me. He brought them to our house.'

As a kid he'd walked in on his father kissing another woman when he'd had no clue what he was seeing. Only that it felt wrong to witness. He'd never wanted to know any of it. He'd been a kid.

'She drowned her hurt in drinking and they fought all the time while maintaining this... supposedly glamorous lifestyle. My dad visited Greece often—keeping up with his friends here, supposedly satisfying Dimitri with his efforts to learn some of the business...but he didn't really care. He brought my mother and me here only the once for my tenth birthday. My mother hated it here. When he got back late one night they had another big fight and he stormed out again. He shouldn't have been driving. The crash killed him instantly. It was lucky there was no one else involved.' He still felt furious with his father for that. 'Dimitri blamed my mother for everything. In his opinion she was why they'd never lived in Greece—because she wasn't Greek. She was the one burning through the money, being unfaithful… Dimitri thought it was all her fault because my father was miserable with her—of course he was going to play up a bit. And then there was me, the reason they'd had to marry in the first place.'

He parked the car outside the villa but sat still, staring through the windscreen, lost in his drive down nightmare lane. 'Dimitri was so angry with her. I overheard him telling her he'd have insisted on a DNA test to prove she hadn't trapped my father with another man's bastard, if it weren't for the fact that I was the spitting image of him. I couldn't stand to hear him talk to her like that when I knew what my father had really been like…'

He'd been torn between defending his mother while burying all the details she'd shared with him. The affairs, the misery and heartache and the rage she'd felt towards his father. Her attempts to make him jealous. All Theo had wanted to do was make her feel better. But he'd failed in that.

'And then, after the funeral, it was time to go home. But my mother said she didn't want me. That she'd never wanted me and that it was best for me to stay with Dimitri.'

'She left you in Greece and returned home to the States?'

He'd begged her to take him with her. Instead she'd signed over all parental rights to Dimitri. A man he'd barely known at the time.

'You must have been heartbroken. You were a *child*.'

He'd been terrified.

'You'd just lost your father, and then your mother too?'

He didn't want her sympathy. He didn't know why he'd told her any of this but now he'd started he couldn't seem to stop. 'The one time I fought Dimitri was when he said something back about her to me. I lost it so badly I thought he was going to...' He breathed in. 'But he didn't. He just never mentioned her name again. I didn't either. We never talk about her or my father. We discuss the business, politics...anything that isn't personal. And it's good. It works.'

That had only changed slightly since Dimitri had got sick and he'd started in on Theo finding a wife.

'Where's your mother now? Are you in contact with her at all?'

He already felt as if he'd been carved open and this memory was like pouring scalding acid on the bleeding wounds, but he couldn't stop the pain—the truth—flowing out. 'A few years ago... I wanted to know where she was, if she was okay...' He'd been a fool to think that, just because he'd made a success of himself, anything would have changed. That she'd want to know him. 'She didn't welcome my visit, didn't want to know. She didn't even want any of my money. She just wanted me to leave her alone. She said her life was better without me. And mine was better without her.'

'Theo—'

'It is better.' He didn't want to hear any different—how could he?

'Is it?'

'Why would I want to revisit it, Leah? My mother was humiliated and hurt and she lashed out. She drowned her sorrows so much that she couldn't stop. My father was beyond miserable too. I can't let anyone else feel that—not Dimitri, not you. I can't let it happen again.'

'Dimitri said he was too hard on you,' she said.

'He told you that?' Shocked, he finally looked at her. 'He's never told me that.'

She looked so serious and concerned. 'Maybe you should talk to him.' She leaned forward to get nearer. 'You should talk to him about what really happened between your parents. Dimitri told me you're different from your father. Maybe he already knows some of it, Theo. You know he's a smart man.'

A smart *business*man, but a blind old fool when it came to his son. Why would Theo ruin that memory for him?

'I wouldn't ever do that.' He rejected the idea immediately, pushing back into his seat. 'He was so hurt by Dad's death. I watched him struggle with grief for so long. Isn't it kinder to leave him believing the good in his son?'

Theo had never wanted to let Dimitri down either. He'd never wanted to do anything that might hurt him—that might make Dimitri push him away.

'He gave me everything I needed—a home, an education, structure and discipline… I owe him, Leah. I can't hurt him.'

'But holding all that in hurts you.'

Now he was looking at her he couldn't seem to look away and that was bad because everything was rising now—all those feelings he'd blocked for years.

'You must have been so lonely.'

And she was right there, looking at him with those compassionate, velvety eyes as everything just slipped from him—the things he'd never said aloud to anyone—and his heart was racing so fast he felt dizzy. 'After a month or so, we went on a boat to Dimitri's holiday home for a weekend. It wasn't like any place I'd ever been to before—I don't mean beautiful buildings, but a place that was a total escape. I was free to roam and swim. It was vast and private and the sea so blue, so warm.' He shook his head as he confessed his last little secret. 'You might have thought it sounded like a prison, but it's always been paradise to me.'

'Oh, Theo—'

At the catch in her whisper he blinked and forced himself to break the connection. He unfastened his belt and got out of the car.

'I should get some food,' he said briskly. 'You must be hungry.' He headed straight into the kitchen.

Anything to change the topic and keep him busy so he wouldn't have to look at her, so he wouldn't give way to that yearning inside compelling him to seek solace in her hold. He couldn't stand to see the empathy in her eyes, or bear the ache it caused.

'You can cook too?' Her laugh sounded strained. 'I don't know why I'm surprised.'

'Actually...' he breathed out, seemingly unable to stop being honest now '... I only have a couple of dishes in my repertoire and they're not great. I just didn't want us to be disturbed.'

He didn't want to have to pretend in front of people.

Maybe that had been a mistake. Maybe having staff around right now might help him reclaim his distance. And perspective. Because the one person he couldn't seem to pretend anything in front of was Leah.

He wasn't even hungry. He didn't know why he was even in the damn kitchen. But she'd opened the fridge and was absently staring at the contents as if she hoped a three-course meal would magically appear if she looked for long enough.

'Don't,' he muttered. He didn't want her waiting on him, helping him, being that kind person who did things for other people all the time. He didn't want her to care for him in the same way she cared for her oldies or in doing nice things for her friends. That wasn't what he wanted. He didn't want anything from her, right? 'You don't have to—'

'Maybe we could just make do,' she interrupted him. 'Pull together a few things picnic style?'

He nodded, unable to argue any more. They briefly worked in silence, but their bodies brushed too close despite the spaciousness of the kitchen. The air almost hummed as his tension built. He sensed hers rising too and that only escalated his. Confusion swirled, twisting into a tornado that he didn't know how to safely release. The silence thickened to the point where he couldn't stand it any more. He stopped what he was doing and stared at her.

She'd stopped too, the moment he had. Her eyes reflected everything—the turmoil, the vulnerable hunger that couldn't be hidden. He couldn't seem to hold anything back from her any more. 'Leah...'

He felt her shudder as he pulled her into his arms. His heart slammed against the palm she placed on his chest and his brain was fried by the look in her eyes as she rose on tiptoe to bring herself closer.

'Maybe we just make do with what we have?' he muttered.

What they had was *this*. With one kiss they

ignited. Desperate to assuage the aching energy that had coiled so unbearably in the course of that conversation, they were wordless now. Swiftly pushing clothes aside, seeking skin, seeking complete contact. He lifted her back onto the big table and with almost no preamble pushed close and hard and deep and it still wasn't enough. She instantly tightened her legs around his waist in response, forming the hottest, tightest vice, and it was as if she were never going to release him. He ground harder, faster, pushing as powerfully as he could, but he still couldn't get close enough. The shocking thing was *this* didn't feel enough any more. That aching hole in his chest hurt—that place where other people had a heart. He growled in agony, in absolute frustration.

But she grabbed his burning face in her hands and kissed him. The passion in her deep caress destroyed that ache in an arc of pure lightning. It wasn't just pleasure branding through his skin and flesh and blood to bone. It was peace and tumultuous contentment and it was perfect. Now it was fiercer than ever. Better than ever.

But now he needed it more than ever.

CHAPTER THIRTEEN

THE FULL MOON bathed the room with pale light even at three in the morning. Still wide awake, Theo tried not to fidget and disturb Leah's sleep but he couldn't rest. He felt flayed, old wounds oozed. That physical bliss had ebbed and allowed cool, biting air—and anxiety—in.

Beside him Leah shifted position, then shifted again. A moment later she left their bed and went into the bathroom.

Theo waited, but the longer she was gone, the more his concern grew. He followed her to knock on the door. 'Leah? You okay?'

She opened the door. She held one hand pressed below her belly button. His senses hit full alert. 'What's wrong?'

She shook her head and rubbed her stomach slightly. 'Nothing.'

It didn't look like nothing. He gazed at her. The soft swell of her belly was bigger now, the secret within her starting to show. Bared like this she was so beautiful, but so very vulnerable.

'You're sore?' He carefully placed his palm just below hers and caressed the curve of her belly. Her skin was so soft and warm he went all the more gently. But mid-sweep he felt a jab against his palm. He stilled and held his palm firm and felt it again—the smallest of punches. It hit him with stupefying power. He glanced up and intercepted her wide-eyed gaze.

'You can feel that?' she breathed.

His throat completely constricted, so he merely nodded mutely.

'It's like this at this time. I think it's got day and night mixed up.' She still whispered, as if afraid speaking would silence the tiny communication.

It? Their baby? Another punch felled those walls that had barely begun their rebuild within him. He was feeling their baby. It was here. Alive and kicking.

He licked his lips and struggled to get his brain back. 'Does it hurt?'

'Not at all.'

'It's…' He didn't know what it was. He didn't know what to say. He didn't know what he was feeling.

'Like something out of a sci-fi movie,' she whispered with a chuckle.

She jolted a smile from him—he could never hold back a smile when she laughed.

'It doesn't seem real, does it?' she whispered.

He shook his head. But it was. *Real.*

He pulled his hand away and motioned for her to get back into bed with him. He held her gently and listened to her breathing, hearing the change as she relaxed and drifted back to sleep. No such bliss for him. Adrenalin coursed through his body. There was a baby on its way. Stupid, but while he'd *known* that, he'd not really *believed* it. He'd not felt it—not literally, like just now. But not inside himself either. Now the fact hit him as if he were being buried in a box by a load of wet cement—he was going to be a father.

And he had no idea how he was going to do that. All he knew was that he didn't want to be like his father. Or even his grandfather—unable to communicate. He never wanted his child to hold in a bottomless well of hurt the way he had.

He wasn't ready. He'd *never* be ready. In fact, he didn't want this at all.

He didn't want the responsibility of his child's happiness weighing on him. He couldn't handle Leah's either. She had her own loves and passions and she should fulfil her own dreams. He couldn't bear it if she ended up *resenting* him... he never should have tied her to him. Yet he couldn't fight that need curling within him to claim them both, protect them both—

Panic pushed his 'problem-solve' button, but the only possible option he could come up with was his original plan. They shouldn't live together. He could ensure their safety and financial security best if he was away from them. He couldn't live with them both and let them down. He couldn't live with *himself* if he did that— especially not now he knew her so well. She deserved better than the little he could provide emotionally and he couldn't stand to see disappointment or disillusionment build in her eyes because of what he lacked. He'd never be able to meet their greatest, deepest needs.

Distance simply had to be restored. Except, at the thought, regret like nothing he'd ever known rose within him.

But Theo was used to holding himself together and doing what was necessary. And this was necessary.

Leah woke and found herself alone again. Her heart dropped—she hated waking without him.

The yearning inside was for more than his touch now; she wanted him to open up to her more. To share more of himself. The hurt he'd faced broke her heart. She'd hardly been able to breathe as he'd told her. And all she'd been able to do was listen, then to hold him. He didn't realise what he gave. Or how much more she wanted.

She found him pacing out by the pool. Her steps slowed as she saw he was already dressed. He looked too smart in his suit and with a remote expression in his eyes. A shard of glass pierced her heart. She knew what he was about to say.

'We need to go back to Athens.'

And there it was. She looked at him and then back at the view towards the mountain behind him. 'Okay.'

Disappointment bloomed within her chest.

'It's work—'

'It's okay,' she repeated.

She didn't want him to explain or try to make excuses. This was the reality and she shouldn't expect more from him. But the last few days had been so lovely—not just their time in Delphi, but leading up to the wedding. She'd had snatches of a future—of dreams and hope for happiness with him.

'I need to work, Leah.'

'Why?' Anger took over the hurt. 'You're supposed to be on your honeymoon.'

'I'm responsible for a lot of people. I can't let them down.'

'Of course.' It was that loyalty and sense of duty again. The relentless drive to do what was right for everyone but himself. 'And you tell me I seek approval too much.' She couldn't hold back the bitter twist to her lips.

'This isn't about seeking anyone's approval—this is about other people's livelihoods.'

'It's always about other people, isn't it, Theo?' She looked at him. 'What about *you*?'

He looked at her. 'You don't need to worry about me.'

'No, you wouldn't want that, would you?' she said. 'Someone to worry about you. Someone to care.'

'I can look after myself, Leah.'

And that was the way he liked it?

He felt duty to many people and for her no more than any other. But she rebelled at that thought. There was more between them than mere sex now and she was sure he felt it too. Yesterday had been the most magical day. She wanted that Theo back—the one who'd let her in. But he'd shut down when he'd felt the baby move. He'd tried to hide it, but he couldn't. He'd not touched her properly since and not talked to her either. Fatherhood was a duty that he was determined to fulfil, but that was all. He didn't actually want it.

'You're back sooner than I thought,' Dimitri greeted them when they landed back at the compound. 'I have a present for you.' He led the way inside, clapping his hands together in almost childlike excitement.

Leah stared. A huge photo of Theo and her from their wedding now hung in pride of place in the centre of that collection of Savas portraits. Leah was aghast.

It was an arty shot, filtered with black and white, but somehow they'd coloured in the silver of her dress…the techniques made her look ethereal and so staggeringly glamorous she couldn't quite believe it was her. And with his sharp suit and solemn visage, Theo looked like a fallen angel. But the appalling thing was their pose—while Theo was staring straight into the camera, her face was turned towards him. She was smiling at him and there was heavenly adoration in her eyes and there was no hiding it from anyone who bothered to look. She didn't want to see Theo's reaction yet she couldn't stop herself staring as he studied the picture. He didn't break that remote countenance and he didn't say a word.

Disconcerted, she glanced at Dimitri and saw the satisfaction in his eyes as he surveyed the portrait. This was what the old man had wanted, wasn't it? Someone to love his grandson. What he didn't realise was that it wasn't enough. Theo had to *want* that love. And he didn't.

She hated disappointing Dimitri almost as much as Theo did. She could understand why he worked so hard to keep the man happy. But the same was true in reverse. Dimitri would do anything for Theo. He was desperate to see him happy and content. They loved each other but they were too lacking in communication skills to admit it. And Theo lacked the trust to be vulnerable enough to share the truth of the past.

So she forced on a smile and faced Dimitri. 'It's beautiful, Dimitri. Thank you.'

He patted her arm and walked through to the lounge, leaving them alone.

'I need to get to the office,' Theo muttered.

'Theo?' It was that huskiness that compelled her to follow him. She followed him out to his

car, pushed past the embarrassment of that portrait. 'Don't go.'

He stopped walking. His broad shoulders
tensed as he pivoted to face her. He didn't want
to have this conversation? Nor did she. But suddenly it was imperative. Somehow she had the
courage. She was done hiding.

'Leah—'

'You don't have to go today. You're choosing
to. Don't avoid me, Theo.' It was so obvious he
was. Just as he avoided Dimitri.

'It's not you, Leah.'

Of course it was. Yes, they had some issues but
they could handle them, couldn't they? But not
if he left. Not if he chose to shut her out again.
She'd thought they'd really communicated, that
he'd really felt something for her…but then he'd
felt the baby and she was scared it had all become too real for him.

'You know what?' She drew in a breath of determination. 'I'm not the same woman you met
that night in London. I've got more confident. I'm
not afraid to wear the colours I like. To say what
I really think. To do whatever it is I want. You
know why? Because just that once, *you* picked
me. And that made me realise other people might
like me too…and that it actually doesn't matter

if they don't. It's okay not to please everyone.' She stepped closer to him. 'You saw me, Theo, and you've believed in me ever since. You've listened to me up till now—please keep listening.'

'Leah—'

'You can't hide that hurt in there for ever.'

An impatient expression flashed in his eyes. 'I knew I shouldn't have—'

'What? Talked to me? What's wrong with opening up to someone? Is it really that awful?' For him, that rejection had run so deep. 'I know you never wanted to marry anyone. I know you were just keeping Dimitri happy when you said you'd meet those women. You weren't intending on going through with any seriously. I know you think you don't want children. You only married me because it was the right thing to do.'

'You claim to know so much, yet you won't accept what I'm incapable of,' he growled at her. 'You need to understand that I cannot be anything more than what I am.' His hands shook at his sides before he clenched them into fists. 'I'm an emotional failure. I couldn't give my mother what she needed. I couldn't meet Dimitri's requirements. I can't meet yours.'

'What requirements do you think I have?' she asked him, desperately trying to understand what he thought she wanted of him. 'I'm in love with *you*, Theo. And *you* know that. That's why you're shutting me out now.'

'No.' He tensed and backed away from her, shaking his head in pure denial. 'You might think you're in love with me. But you're not.'

He didn't believe her? His doubt slammed her momentum to a halt.

'I shouldn't have slept with you again.' Turning away, he shakily ruffled a hand through his hair.

She was appalled. 'You think you've been trifling with my emotions?' Did he not accept how *real* this was?

'Of course I have. You've not had…'

'Any other lovers?' she finished for him. 'No, I haven't. But that doesn't make me an idiot, Theo. Don't treat me like someone who doesn't know her own mind, her own body, her own feelings.'

He closed his eyes momentarily. 'Even if you mean them, I can't carry that burden.'

'It's a *gift*,' she pleaded with him to understand. 'Not a life sentence. It's light. Love, laughter, support.'

'No, it's not. You cannot deny there's a responsibility on me. On my actions. I need to be careful because you're vulnerable.'

'All you have to do is act like a *human*. Not be cruel. You don't have to love me back.'

'Good, because I can't return those feelings. Not ever.'

She flinched. His words hit her heart like burning-hot bullets. Was it only her? Or was it anybody who tried to get close who he pushed away?

'I know you don't want to be hurt,' she said to him again, softly—more hesitant now. 'I'm so sorry your parents were unhappy, but that wasn't your fault.'

'How can you say that?' he roared. 'They were only together because of me. They fought because of me. He died because of me.'

'They were adults. They made choices. It was never *you*.'

'Of course it was me.' He rolled his shoulders. 'She never wanted me.' He glanced at her. 'And that's okay. Look at me properly, Leah—do I look like someone who's struggling? I'm *fine*. I'm happy. I like my life as it is and I don't need you—' He broke off, his breathing sharp.

She shook her head, refusing to believe his rejection. 'You told me it wasn't my fault I couldn't live up to my parents' expectations. Why isn't it the same for you? Why take the blame for their incompatibility? You were the innocent.

You're not responsible for everyone and everything. It's not down to you to protect us all—not this baby, not Dimitri, not me.' She gazed at him. 'Maybe it's just fate? Maybe we just lucked out with the parent thing. But you know what? We can't change it—we can only accept it. And we have to appreciate what's really good. *We're* good, Theo. You and me. And I'm not going to raise this baby the way my mother raised me. We're not them, Theo.'

'No. And I know you'll be a wonderful mother. But I'm still not capable of being what *you* want, Leah.'

'You already *are* what I want. Just as you are.'

He jerked his head and his gaze dropped. 'I can't give your baby—'

His voice cracked.

'*Our* baby,' she whispered.

'Stop,' he snapped, fury unleashed. 'Just stop. I have *tried,* Leah. But this? It's never going to happen. You ask too much.'

She stared at him. He meant it, he really meant it. And she suddenly knew there was nothing she could say to change his mind. He didn't think he could be enough for her.

'I get that you don't want this from me.' She breathed carefully so she could still speak. 'But you should talk to Dimitri, Theo. You should be as honest with him. Because you *do* love him.'

She might've been wrong to read anything more into their relationship, but she was certain about that.

'I can't.' His chest rapidly rose and fell and he spun away from her, yanking open the car door. 'I have to go.'

Leah stood still as his car roared off into the distance, shocked by the rejection buffeting her soul. She'd pushed him too far—asked for things he'd never wanted to give. Or at least, not to her. Should she just have done as he wanted, without saying anything? Should she have stayed silent and kept it all in?

No. That was what he did and look how well that worked.

Her invisibility was ended and the bittersweet irony was because that was thanks to *him*. He'd turned her life upside down all those months ago. But those changes had begun from that one magical night. He'd injected a confidence within her and she'd held that memory close. It had been like a bubble inflating her heart. And while he'd just stomped on it, it wasn't going anywhere. She wouldn't let his rejection destroy her; she wouldn't revert to the person she'd been before meeting him.

She'd come too far. And what she'd asked for hadn't been too much. It hadn't been anything more than she deserved. It was what everyone deserved—to be loved, wholly and completely and unconditionally. For a few magical moments he'd made her feel as if she could have it all. They were good together in so many ways. But he was under no obligation to give her anything more than what he'd originally offered… if he didn't care for her. He didn't. But her heart ached, her whole body ached…because she so badly wanted to believe he did.

She desperately wanted to run away, but she refused to. She wasn't doing that to her baby. Nor to Dimitri. Not even to Theo. None of them deserved that. They all—including her—deserved a family. And they'd make one—though it might not end up being particularly conventional. She'd do everything she could to ensure her child received love from both its parents. Because he would love this baby, she knew he would, even if he couldn't yet believe that of himself.

But she had to cope with her own heartbreak too. She had to get away from him to do that. The only solution she could see was for her to go to his island holiday home as he'd suggested from the start. Theo could work in Athens, keep an eye on Dimitri and whatever else he needed and she could avoid him.

It wasn't his fault he hadn't fallen in love with her the way she had with him. But she couldn't stand to stay another night with him. She certainly couldn't sleep with him again. *That* would destroy her. And she couldn't trust herself around him. He couldn't have absolutely everything from her because she *did* deserve more.

To preserve herself, she had to leave now.

CHAPTER FOURTEEN

THEO ROLLED HIS shoulders as he walked across the terrace. Dimitri was sitting by the pool, with a pile of reading material on the table beside him and one of Leah's blankets draped over his knees. He looked tired and his eyes held only a shadow of the warmth that had been there this morning when Theo had returned with Leah.

'You've been doing too much again.' Theo frowned as he saw the tinge of greyness in the old man's face. 'You're still supposed to take it easy.'

He looked towards the house, his chest tightening at the prospect of seeing Leah. The words she'd so passionately declared had echoed in his mind all day. Going to work had been pointless other than to simply escape her. But he couldn't even do that—his mind had replayed the moment over and over. She'd stood there with such dignity like a tall, slender tree. And he'd cut her down.

He wanted to kick himself. He'd been such a fool to think he could have any kind of relationship with her. He'd known, hadn't he, right from the start that she was gentler than most? She'd been a virgin, for heaven's sake. No one had made her feel special or wanted before—of course she thought she'd developed feelings for him. He braced, holding off seeing her. Was she still hiding upstairs? Still crying? Was she too upset to sit with Dimitri and stumble over a few Greek words while working on a new pattern? He hated the thought of her being distraught.

It finally dawned on him that the place felt too silent.

'You worked late,' Dimitri muttered.

'There was a lot of work that needed doing,' he replied. And it had taken him three times as long because his concentration was shot.

I'm in love with you.

He shook off the memory. Again.

'You've been married less than a week,' Dimitri commented.

Theo didn't answer.

The reality of last night had given him every reason to keep his distance. But the desire to see her, just to see, was too strong. It wasn't sexual desire, it was concern. Just concern. He needed a glimpse to ensure she was okay. Then he'd retreat.

'Leah?' he called out as he entered the house, holding back the desire to run.

She didn't reply.

Unease scraped down his spine. He gave up on his restraint and ran up the stairs, taking two at a time. 'Leah?'

He walked into their room. It felt emptier. He suddenly realised the whole house felt emptier. Suspicion ballooned and he glanced in the wardrobe. Her eveningwear was still there, but those pairs of jeans, those tees, were gone. He pulled open the first of the drawers in her stand. Her silky, scarlet smalls were gone.

She was gone.

He froze, trying to process it. Then panic hit. Where had she gone? Was she okay? Why?

But he knew why. He knew exactly why. He'd hurt her.

He raced back downstairs just as Dimitri came into the house.

'What's wrong?' The old man watched him.

'I think she's left me.' He could hardly breathe as he strode past Dimitri to double-check the lounge.

'Pardon?'

'Leah. She's gone.' His anger leaked.

'Pardon?' Dimitri glowered at him.

'What part of "left me" don't you understand?' he stormed back as rage blew him apart.

'You're the one who doesn't understand,' Dimitri growled. 'You think she's left you? Is that what Leah would really do?'

Theo froze, then whirled to glare at his grandfather. 'Do you know where she is? Why didn't you tell me?'

'Why didn't you ask?'

'I don't have time for games, Dimitri. Where is she?' He needed to know she was okay.

'Why leave her alone all day? Bored and lonely with no one but an old man for company.'

'You're not that old and this place isn't boring.' He drew in a breath. 'I don't have time for this. I'll get Philip to help find her. She can't have gone far.'

'Philip is with her.'

'What?'

'She's gone to the island.'

Theo reached out and pressed his fingers to the wall to balance himself as he gaped at Dimitri. 'She what?'

'She said that was what you wanted.'

She hadn't run away? She wasn't alone out

there in Athens, checking herself into some boarding house or something? She wasn't on a plane back to England?

Relief was like a blissfully cool balm soothing the rawness inside but then that very balm began to heat, burning his wounds worse. He'd thought she'd chosen to vanish—to run and hide from him completely because she'd been hurt. But she hadn't—she'd simply done as he'd originally asked.

He slumped against the wall, his legs empty of all strength. 'Okay. Okay, good.'

It was good, wasn't it? It was what he'd wanted. It would make things simple. So why did he feel worse than he had when he'd thought she was missing?

'You're not going there now?' Dimitri looked confused.

'No.' He drew a breath. 'I'll check in with Philip on the phone. There's no need for me to go.'

'I sent Amalia with her.' Dimitri's mouth thinned. 'To care for her.'

The unspoken criticism hung heavy. Theo rejected it. 'Thank you,' he said curtly.

He turned his back to avoid his grandfather's colossal disapproval. Flashes of memory tortured him as he climbed the stairs towards terrible privacy—her laughter that night in the theatre foyer, her latent playfulness, her humour and kindness. But all that warmth was lost to him. Because Theo *couldn't* care for her. He couldn't give what she needed. He'd always known she'd be better off away from him. And so would his child.

But he wasn't better off. Three long, hellish days and nights later he was nothing but worse. Nothing but angry. Nothing but poison. He missed her. And he hated that he missed her. He hated that she had got to him in a way no one ever had. That she'd made him want things. Things he was so afraid of losing that it was easier not to have had them in the first place.

'You need to rest.' He watched Dimitri silently push his dinner around his plate. The old man looked frailer than ever.

'How's Leah?' Dimitri asked.

He couldn't answer. He didn't know.

'I don't like to see you like this,' Dimitri added with a belligerent edge.

Like what? He wasn't the one who looked as if he was about to keel over.

Theo shovelled a bite of food into his mouth and chewed, tasting nothing.

'I didn't think you'd do this.'

Theo looked sharply at Dimitri. He recognised that low throb of anger. He just knew the rarely voiced criticism that was coming—Dimitri was about to blame his mother.

'That you'd be like—'

'I'm nothing like *him*,' he snapped. 'I'd never treat Leah the way my *father* treated my *mother*.' He instantly sucked in a breath but it was too late to pull the words back.

Dimitri flinched and turned ashen.

'I'm sorry,' Theo muttered, dropping his fork with a clatter. 'I didn't—'

'Don't be sorry,' Dimitri interrupted firmly, despite his complexion. 'Tell me.'

Conflicted, Theo froze. But he remembered Leah's entreaty for him to speak honestly with Dimitri. And he remembered that easing inside when he'd talked to *her*. He ached to talk to her like that again and, thanks to her, he finally realised he ought to with his grandfather too. 'I don't want to hurt you.'

'I know my son was not a saint,' Dimitri said. 'I know they both suffered.'

'I think maybe they brought the worst out in each other.'

'And you were caught between them.'

'No,' Theo sighed. 'They just didn't care, Papou.'

The pet name for his grandfather slipped out. And then all the secrets slipped—snatches of truth and hurt tumbled free, the memories that had cut most deeply. Dimitri put his hand on his shoulder and just listened and somehow Theo told him even more—even about that awful trip to see his mother. All the things he'd held back for so long because he hadn't wanted to hurt him. But Dimitri's low growl wasn't an expression of pain for himself, but empathy for Theo. There was no changing any of it, Theo understood that. But in sharing there was acknowledgement and acceptance and finally forgiveness—of those parents who just hadn't had it in them to be there for him. And it was, he finally believed, something lacking in *them*, rather than something missing in him.

'I'm proud of you, Theo.' Gruff and awkward, Dimitri shook him in a fumbling hug. 'I want to see you happy. I want to see Leah happy.'

'So do I.' Theo buried his face in his hands. 'But I...'

'What's worse?' his grandfather asked simply. 'The thought of life with her? Or without?'

CHAPTER FIFTEEN

FIVE DAYS.

No contact.

He'd not called, not left any messages, not visited. There'd been nothing. And that was a good thing. Because Leah was getting on with it.

Amalia was staying with her in the main villa while a security guard stayed in the gatehouse at the edge of the property. Leah knew the older woman was worried about her. But she needn't be. Things were fine. How could they not be when she now lived in this breathtaking place with its crisply white, curved buildings and stunning clear blue waters? The view was unbelievable—all sea, all sky. Every day she watched the sun rise and then later set, a beautiful blinding blaze set against that backdrop of brilliant blue. It was gorgeously warm, sweet and spicy wild herbs scented the air and she'd never known a place as perfect could exist. Theo had been right.

But the beauty broke her heart all the more,

because it was something that screamed to be shared.

But there'd be no wallowing in bed and weeping. During the day, her determination held. She swam in the pool or at the private beach, then walked to the nearby village. Initially she'd greeted the locals with only a smile and a smattering of her appalling Greek but already a few of the women now stopped to talk for longer. Theo had been right about that too.

When she returned to the villa, she worked on plans. At first it had been purely for distraction. But as she'd thought about it more, a tiny spark had flared and now she was all in. Theo had been right to get her thinking more about that was well. Why shouldn't she create some kind of business with her knitting and pattern designs? Some kind of community? Her enthusiasm for that consumed the daylight hours.

But the tears came in the small hours when she was too tired and sleepless and sad to stop them. The loneliness was like nothing she'd experienced because she'd had a glimpse of what could've been. She missed him on so many levels. He'd made more than just her body come alive; he'd made her laugh. He'd been fun, intelligent, attentive and so caring, even though he couldn't see that in himself.

But he'd not been effortlessly falling into love the way she had. And she was not going to lie—that *hurt*. She couldn't want love from someone unable—and unwilling—to give it. She couldn't stay, knowing she wasn't enough for the person she wanted that unconditional love from. It had been hard enough being a disappointment to her parents.

At least Theo hadn't *lied*. And who was she to try to change him?

Every time a helicopter swept overhead she stiffened with nerves. Would he ever come see her or was he going to ignore her for ever? There'd been no helicopters at all today. The sun was high and she'd got too hot even in the shade outside, so she'd gone to her bedroom to try to catch up on some of the sleep that had been eluding her.

So far, no sleep.

At a movement in the doorway, she glanced up, expecting it to be Amalia, with one of the delicious treat trays she regularly brought her. But it wasn't Amalia.

Theo stepped into her room—tall, serious, *devastating*.

Her heart whacked so hard and fast against her ribcage she put her fist to her chest to hold it inside.

'What are you doing here?' She scrambled off the bed.

She'd thought she was getting on top of her feelings, but in a flash they were all back, all-consuming. Elation. Desolation. It was far too soon to see him. It was always going to be too soon. And her bedroom was too intimate a space.

'Leah.'

How could she collapse so completely when all he did was look at her like that and say her name? She clenched her teeth, willing herself to stay strong and in control.

'What do you want?' she asked defensively as he stood watching her every move.

'I can't visit you?'

'Not unannounced, no.' She squared her shoulders. It was time to set the rules she needed in place to survive this.

His gaze didn't waver and that green deepened. 'But we're married.'

'We're not a normal married couple.' To her horror her voice weakened.

Because they were never going to be that. He didn't want that.

He still didn't move, yet somehow he seemed nearer. 'How are you finding prison island?'

She wanted to scream her heartache at him. She wanted to hate him for it. But she was so unprepared for seeing him again and the last thing she felt was hate. 'It's beautiful,' she said.

To her surprise something that looked like anger flared in his eyes.

'Really?' His soft query was laced with a lethal edge. 'So you're going to be happy here?'

She stared in disbelief that he'd asked that. Her anger burned closer to the surface. 'Don't you want me to be happy?'

Another expression flickered across his face but he swiftly stiffened and she couldn't even try to read it.

'It's better for us to live apart,' she said firmly. He'd been right.

But he didn't say anything, he just kept looking at her as if he couldn't believe she was in front of him, as if he were afraid that if he so much as blinked she might disappear. And it wasn't fair of him to look at her like *that*.

'What do you want from me, Theo?' she flared. She was trying to give him what he'd wanted. '*Why* are you here? The baby's not due for a few months. Can't you just leave me alone and let me deal with—?'

She broke off, not wanting to name the blistering emotions steamrollering through her.

'After you first left...' His voice was so croaky it faded away.

She watched as he visibly fought for control.

'I thought I'd come and tell you it was all okay, that you should go back to Britain if you wanted. I'd set you up and pay for everything and come visit you and the baby when it suits you...but I don't want you to do that.'

Pain welled inside her. 'I wouldn't want to. The baby needs you. You need the baby too.' Because that was true. He might not think he had anything more to offer their child than financial security, but he did. 'That's why I'm here.'

But she pressed her lips together, not admitting her own need of him. He didn't want that.

He watched her, waiting, as if he knew there was more she wanted to say but couldn't.

'It's not the baby I need, Leah,' he muttered jerkily. 'It's you.'

Painful tears blinded her and she shook her head.

'Leah?'

'No.' She turned away, because she couldn't believe him. 'No, Theo.'

Somehow he was right there, his hands on her shoulders, pressing with firm but gentle pressure to get her to turn back to face him.

She ached to resist. But she still didn't have the strength. 'Please...' She broke off and closed her eyes to hold back those burning tears. But they slipped free anyway, tracking down her cheeks.

'Leah.' His thread of a voice broke. 'I'm so sorry.'

She sucked in a shaky breath. 'You don't need to be sorry. It's okay. I'm okay.' This was going to be fine. 'You just need to stay away and let me get on with it for a while.'

'You really meant it.' A whisper—of disbelief, of regret, of sorrow.

That she loved him? 'Of course I did.'

He was gazing into her eyes and she couldn't look away now because he was looking at her with such anguish. 'I'm sorry I didn't know how to accept that gift, Leah. I'm so sorry. No one's given me that before. And that it was you?' He shook his head. 'It meant too much. You'd given me something so fragile—like burning, just-blown glass—and I was too scared to take hold of it in case I warped it somehow. In case it really was nothing more than a bubble that would burst if I even breathed. I just didn't know how to handle it.'

She stilled, unsure she could believe what she thought he was trying to say.

'I'm mucking this up.' He groaned and moved closer still. 'I'm not okay, Leah. I'm not fine. I miss you.'

'But this is what you wanted.' There was a lump in her chest as if she'd swallowed a giant jagged piece of ice.

'I think I've been afraid for so long that I forgot I even was. It's just normal. I didn't even recognise I'd put defences in place. That afternoon when I came home and found out you'd gone I didn't realise you'd come here. I thought you'd left for good.'

'I could never do that to you. I couldn't hide your child from you. Not knowing you the way I—'

'I know, sweetheart. I know and I'm sorry. It was so stupid of me. I'm not great at understanding love, Leah.' He nodded. 'And I know you're used to feeling hurt by those who should show you the greatest care. But you shouldn't be. You deserve so much more than that.'

She swallowed.

'I used my parents as an excuse to keep you away. I didn't want to care. I didn't think I actually could. But, Leah, I've fallen for you. From that very first night, I just couldn't let myself recognise it.'

She shook her head. 'No.'

He tensed, his eyes widening. 'No?'

'Not from that first night,' she muttered. 'It's all…circumstance. If it weren't for this baby, we wouldn't have seen each other again.'

'I don't think that's true.'

'Of course it is—'

'How did I know where to find you?' he interrupted. 'When I came to London after you walked into the bank, how did I find you?'

'You…used your magical too-much-money powers to track down my address.'

'Yes, that's exactly what I did. But do you know *when* I did that?'

'After I called into the office…'

'No. I had my team put together a report on you the day I returned to Greece. The day after we spent the night together.'

She stared at him. Right after that? 'But you didn't do anything with it.'

He swallowed. 'I dreamed of you. But I thought I was doing the right thing for both of us.'

'Because I'm not—'

'Because I have this stupid terror inside that I couldn't get past. Not until you came back and lit up my world. Until you then left and I realised how horrendous life is without you. How much I want and need you in it because I love you. I'm so sorry I've hurt you and that I let you go. I never should have done that. Have I ruined this completely, Leah?'

She was reeling inside. She had to take this chance; she had to have a playful moment. 'Not completely.'

He suddenly smiled.

'Keep talking.' Her heart pounded but she couldn't stop a little laugh of disbelief and delight escaping. 'Just keep talking.'

'Come home with me.' That old assurance sounded in his voice again.

'Why?' She needed more, she needed to hear it again and again. But she cupped his face in her hands as he asked.

'Because I love you. I miss you. I want you. I need you,' he confessed, leaning closer as he too struggled to breathe. 'Everything I never thought I'd say. Never thought I'd feel. I want it all with you, Leah.'

His gaze blazed with such intimate intensity and truth she almost couldn't bear it.

'Theo—'

He kissed her—as if he couldn't resist any more. As if he'd run out of words and only action was left to convince her, as if he couldn't get enough of her, as if she were the most precious thing in the world, breathlessly, brokenly. His whole body shook against hers, as if he was trying to go gently, but the strength of his need kept slipping through resulting in a soul-breaking, star-bursting kiss that she wanted never to end.

'Don't let go of me.' Tears sprang to her eyes again. 'Please don't ever let go of me.'

'Never. Never again. I'm so sorry.'

She was home in his arms. His grip on her tightened and he kissed her again. Everything was unleashed now—uncontrollable, unstoppable—the need to touch, to possess, to connect was too strong. Hands swept—clutching, touching, taking.

'I missed you,' he growled raggedly. 'Missed you so much.'

She trembled as he pinned her, kissing her, caressing every inch as if he desperately needed to rediscover her every secret. Every want.

But then he slowed as he gently stroked her

belly. 'This scares me.' He glanced up, hot, raw honesty tumbling from him. 'But it brought you back into my life and for that I will always adore it.' He kissed that soft curve and looked up at her again, vulnerability visible in the sheen of his eyes. 'I'm going to need your help. I don't know how to be a husband…as for a father…'

'We'll figure it out together,' she promised him, her throat so tight she could hardly speak.

'Make do with what we have?' A half-smile broke his strain.

She nodded and curled herself about him, holding him where she needed him—with her, sealed along every inch. 'Together, we have everything.'

They had such ecstasy. And it was so sublime she actually laughed as he claimed her—her joy was too intense to be contained. He smiled back—she loved his smile. Loved him. Loved *this* with him.

And then she couldn't laugh any more, she couldn't speak. She—like he—could only *show*. In every kiss, every caress, there was total love.

Later, cuddled close, she never wanted either of them to move again. But Theo wriggled; reaching down to the floor, he scooped up his jeans and got something out of the pocket before lying back beside her. He put the small box he'd retrieved on her stomach and then took her hand and slid the diamond ring from her finger.

'What are you doing?' she asked, but she couldn't move in case that other little box slipped off her skin.

He held the diamond in his hand for a moment before placing it on the bedside table. 'I've regretted giving you this ring from the moment I did.' He shot her a smile at her barely stifled gasp of dismay. 'I thought if I kept everything impersonal, I could keep you at a distance. But you were already under my skin. I didn't choose that diamond. I didn't want to think about what you might like. I didn't want to think of you at all. But it was all I ended up doing. The more I wanted to hold you away, the more you flooded me—filling all those dark, empty corners, Leah.' He picked up the box on her stomach. 'I spent the last week thinking about everything I'd do differently and this is the smallest of the things that I can do differently. I chose this one—your favourite colour…not so secret any more.' His smile was a touch self-conscious.

The ruby was so richly coloured it was almost crimson. Flanked by square-cut diamonds, it was sensual and striking and her eyes burned with its beauty. She shook her head as the tears threatened again.

'You don't like it?' He actually looked anxious. 'We can change it. You can choose—'

'No.' She put her fingers on his lips, half laughing, half crying. 'It's beautiful, I love it.'

Not only because it was stunning, but because of what it signified. He wanted to please her. But that in itself made her panic again. 'But you know you don't have to give me things. I don't want you feeling like you have to please me...' She breathed shakily. 'You've spent so long trying to please, trying to be perfect just in case—'

'And you haven't?' He cupped her jaw. 'You *do* things for people, Leah. For everyone—your friends, family... You did things for me too— you wore those heels and drove me mad. But this is different. It's not only to please you, but me too. Because I love you like I've never loved anyone. I never knew it was possible. And it's scary and wonderful and I just want to give you everything.'

'The only everything I need is you. Just you.'

He leaned over her, mischief sparkling in his gaze. 'So you don't want the ring?'

She hesitated, loving his flash of humour. And

she slowly smiled. 'Maybe we should just see how it looks.'

He pushed the ring down her finger until it nestled next to the wedding band and they both laughed. He looked into her eyes. 'Perfect.'

She nodded. 'Want to know what else would be perfect right now?'

'Oh, I already do.' His hands slid to where they were so sweetly welcome. 'Mine to have and hold.'

'For ever.' She'd never felt as content and secure and as loved.

'I never want to spend another night apart from you.' He trailed his fingers up and down her arm. 'We need to speak to Dimitri,' he said with a smile in his voice. 'He and I talked.'

'Really?'

'You were right. He'd guessed some, I told him more. He was sad but he was mostly concerned about me. And you.' He suddenly smiled. 'You're like this hot marshmallow, fitting perfectly between us to forge us into a real family. You've made us both melt. You're like the sweetest glue…'

'You think I'm a hot marshmallow?' She chuckled, but inside *she* was the one melting.

'So hot.' He nodded. 'And he'll be thrilled to see you come home with me.'

'We'll come back here often though, won't we?'

He sent her a look of total triumph and pleasure. 'You really like it?'

'You were right. Not prison. Paradise.' She looked at him, overwhelmed with emotion to see him looking so happy. That he felt as deeply for her? 'I love you so much it hurts.'

'I don't want it to hurt, Leah.' He swiftly kissed her, his arms tightening like bars around her. She was imprisoned in the paradise that was his love.

Perfect, profound peace settled deep into her heart. 'I think, as long you're holding me, it won't.'

CHAPTER SIXTEEN

Three years later

LEAH WATCHED THE helicopter descending over the island and put her sketchbook down. She'd not made much progress on her latest design today, too distracted waiting for this—Theo's return. There was a shriek from the other side of the pool where her daughter, Petra, had been dangling her feet in the water while her great-grandfather, Dimitri, read to her. Petra too knew what the helicopter meant.

While Theo never spent more than a night away from them unless he absolutely had to, he'd had to stay in Athens for a couple of days. Now, pulse skipping, Leah watched until he appeared around the corner from the helipad. His sleeves were rolled back and Leah's stomach flipped in that funny way it did when she saw him again. Three years of marriage, of making love every night, hadn't cured her helpless desire for him.

Instead it had deepened and today the butterflies in her tummy were as skittish as that very first night they'd met. But as he moved across the terrace with that purposeful stride, it wasn't only Leah who was captivated by his appearance.

'Daddy!'

Laughing, he dropped his bag and crouched down as Petra ran towards him. Leah's heart swelled as he scooped their toddler up and swung her into his embrace. Petra's squeals of delight rang clear across the azure pool. Leah's eyes filled. Her lovely little girl had a father who adored her and was so demonstrative about it. He was everything Leah had ever wanted and he gave everything she could ever have wished for to their child—total, unconditional love. He gave that to her too. They'd learned together.

Summer on the island was sheer bliss. Her little family spent long, lazy days here, enjoying the sea and the sun and sheer fun of being together. In the last couple of years, Dimitri's health hadn't just stabilised, he'd been reinvigorated thanks to Petra. The little girl filled all their hearts till they overflowed, forcing them to beat stronger still.

Her brother had visited and they'd defrosted him from the lab. He'd then returned—coming at least a couple of times a year, which was wonderful. They'd seen her parents on one of their trips to England but didn't spend too much time with them. It hurt Leah less now she had too much else in her life to treasure.

With Theo's encouragement Leah had pressed forward with the plans she'd begun while they'd been apart for those terrible few days. She now owned an online knitwear company, but, as she had no real need to turn a profit, she'd established it as a charitable enterprise. For every item purchased, a second item was donated to those in need—they'd made and given children's jumpers, wool blankets, ballet crossovers for a dance school offering free classes in an underprivileged area in London… There were so many to help and she loved it. What was more, over a surprisingly short time she'd developed a really active online community who provided laughter and support for her venture. She'd begun selling her pattern designs and they'd become popular too so now she spent most of her work hours designing and knitting up samples…from beautiful baby shawls and cosy natural blankets to luxury silk sweaters and, of course, the original ultimate outrageous leg warmers. But right now, the thought of handling anything woollen seemed mad—she was hot inside and out from studying her too-stunning husband, waiting for the right moment to tell him her secret.

He called something to Dimitri and murmured something else to Petra, who smiled and ran back to her great-grandfather, who picked up the book again. Theo then casually grabbed his bag and turned towards Leah.

Finally.

Their gazes locked. Even from across the pool she sensed the heat flare within him, matching that which was building inside her. But she remained still as he slowly sauntered over to where she reclined in the shade. There was no denying it, right now she was living like some spoiled minor Greek goddess...and she loved it. He made her feel utterly adored. That familiar spark radiated from deep within her, igniting the need that always sat so close to her surface. He hadn't released her gaze and now he smiled a slow wicked smile. Her heart raced even faster.

'You're pleased to see me, *agape mou*,' he murmured.

She'd been counting down the hours more desperately than ever today. But she didn't bother to reply, instead she leaned forward and lifted her face towards him. He slid his hand to the nape of her neck and drew closer. His kiss was leisurely and thorough to the point that her toes curled. Luscious, loving and yet not enough.

'How was your day?' He sat on the edge of her lounger and she shifted her legs to make more room for him.

'Good,' she breathed. It was even better now he was back and still had his hand resting on her shoulder. 'Though I fell asleep this afternoon.' She giggled. 'Poor Petra was showing me her dancing skills but the music was dreamy and I just drifted away.'

'Hmm. You've been tired lately.' Something smouldered in his eyes.

A swirl of tension drew her closer. 'You've noticed that?' She licked her lips.

'I've noticed a few other things as well.' He traced a finger from her shoulder along the edge of her V-necked tee to rest at the top of her cleavage.

Her already oversensitive breasts tightened even more beneath his blatant inspection.

'Maybe with all this time on the island, I'm getting lazy.' She grabbed his hand to stop him teasing, but held it close to her chest. Her heart thudded harder.

'Maybe.' He cocked his head and sounded disbelieving, but his smile deepened.

'Too many late nights working on my new design?' she offered, but she sounded too breathless to pull it off properly and she had to look away from him and stifle her giggle.

'Maybe, but then, the last few nights you've been going to bed earlier than usual.' He bent closer. 'So maybe there's another reason.'

'Low iron?' She peeped a look at him from under her lashes.

He flicked his eyebrows, heightening that sinfully amused look. 'It's not that, Leah…'

She bit her lip, trying to hold back her giveaway laughter. 'What do you think it is?'

He chuckled delightedly. 'Perhaps I know you better than you know yourself.'

'You think…?'

He opened his bag and pulled out a box. 'You want to prove me right?' He presented the home pregnancy test to her.

Leah laughed and took the box from him with her thumb and index finger, only to swivel and drop it to the ground with a flourish.

'I don't need to, because I did one early this morning.' She couldn't hold back her joy and she leaned forward, threw her arms around his neck and all but sobbed, 'I'm pregnant!'

'I *knew* it,' he growled, swiftly seizing her by the waist and pulling her right onto his lap.

'At the *same time* as me, thank you very much,' she said with a squeak but tightened her hold back on him.

He kissed her again.

It was only when the gurgling laughter from their daughter across the pool impinged that he pulled back. Leah rested her forehead against his and looked into his brilliant eyes, unable to stop smiling. The love she felt for him? The connection they had?

'Leah,' he murmured.

She heard the depth in his voice, saw it in his eyes—he felt it the same.

'What you've done for Dimitri and me? The gift that is Petra, and now this baby?' He looked so happy. 'You've given me everything. Now I know how to love, how to be loved…and I *love* you.'

She leaned closer, resting against him—with him—so beautifully content.

* * * * *

LET'S TALK
Romance

For exclusive extracts, competitions
and special offers, find us online:

f facebook.com/millsandboon

⊙ @millsandboonuk

🐦 @millsandboon

Or get in touch on 0844 844 1351*

For all the latest titles coming soon,
visit millsandboon.co.uk/nextmonth

*Calls cost 7p per minute plus your phone company's price per
minute access charge

Want even more
ROMANCE?

Join our bookclub today!